THE QUOKKA QUESTION

THE QUOKKA QUESTION

A Kylie Kendall Mystery

BY
CLAIRE
MCNAB

alyson books
NEW YORK

Celebrating Twenty-Five Years

MANUFACTURED IN THE UNITED STATES OF AMERICA.

PUBLISHED BY ALYSON BOOKS,
P.O. BOX 1253, OLD CHELSEA STATION, NEW YORK, NEW YORK 10113-1251.
DISTRIBUTION IN THE UNITED KINGDOM BY TURNAROUND PUBLISHER SERVICES LTD.,
UNIT 3, OLYMPIA TRADING ESTATE, COBURG ROAD, WOOD GREEN,
LONDON N22 6TZ ENGLAND.

ISBN 0-7394-6596-1
ISBN-978-0-7394-6596-7

CREDITS
COVER ILLUSTRATION BY NICK STADLER.
COVER DESIGN BY MATT SAMS.

For Sheila, muse extraordinaire

Many thanks to Arthur Winer for his expertise

ONE

"G'day," I said, holding out my hand. I felt a thrill of anticipation. I was about to take on my second real case at Kendall & Creeling Investigative Services. "I'm Kylie Kendall. And you must be Dr. Oscar Braithwaite."

"Oscar will do."

"Then you must call me Kylie."

The bloke in the crumpled brown suit standing on the other side of my desk leaned over to shake my hand. I retrieved my crushed fingers and gestured for him to take a seat.

After carefully aligning a yellow writing pad on my desk, I picked up a pen and looked alert. "You mentioned on the phone, Oscar, that your problem was something to do with the quokka question. Just what is the question about quokkas?"

Oscar Braithwaite sat back in the chair as though I'd said something out of turn. Actually, I was making an educated guess at his reaction, because his expression was hard to discern. The lower half of his face was concealed by an untidy mustache and beard that seemed never to have been trimmed. His brown hair was similarly wild, and almost hid his eyes. The only feature I could see clearly was his bulbous nose, and it didn't tell me much about his inner feelings.

"I don't imagine you even know what a 'quokka' is," he said, not unkindly. He had a raspy voice, sounding like it was rusty from lack of use, which was entirely possible, as I'd gathered he spent most of his time alone in the Aussie bush peering at the wildlife.

"I've never seen one," I said, "but I know they're some sort of a

1

cousin to wallabies. They're little hopping marsupials living on an island off the coast of Western Australia."

Maybe he was surprised at my knowledge. I couldn't tell. "Rottnest Island," he said. "There are also some quokka colonies on the south-western mainland, but not many."

There was a knock at the door, and my partner in the business entered, her usual stunning self in tight black pants and black silk shirt. "Dr. Braithwaite? I'm Ariana Creeling."

One look from Ariana's laser-blue eyes, and this bloke was putty in her mitts. I had a fair idea how he felt. He shot to his feet and shook hands with her, showing far more enthusiasm than he'd had when greeting me. "Very pleased to meet you!" he exclaimed.

I admired the way Ariana didn't wince when he squeezed her fingers but maintained her usual reserved expression. "Do you mind if I sit in?" she asked him.

"No, of course not." Somewhere in all that hair I detected a grin. "I'll get you a seat."

While Oscar collected a chair from the other side of the room, Ariana said to me, "Bob's been delayed."

"Right-oh."

Although I'd inherited a controlling share of Kendall & Creeling from my dad, I was only an apprentice P.I., and Bob Verritt oversaw everything I did. When he wasn't there, Ariana took his place. Since Oscar Braithwaite had specifically asked for me, it had become my case, but a licensed private investigator had to monitor me.

Oscar sat down next to Ariana. I had the sense he was beaming at her. To drag his attention back to business, I said, "I meant to ask, Oscar, how you came to hear of Kendall & Creeling."

"You've made a bit of a splash, back home, Kylie. I saw you on the telly. Being pretty sure I was going to need a P.I. when I hit Los Angeles, I took a note of your name."

"Dinkum? I've been on television?" I wondered why no one in my hometown of Wollegudgerie had told me about it. "What was the program?"

He shrugged. "Some sort of newsmagazine thing—'Aussie Chicks

Make Good,' I think it was called."

"Oh," I said, thinking this wasn't necessarily the national exposure one would hope for. I was all set to ask him for more details—after all, this was my first appearance on television—but Ariana gave me a get-on-with-it look. "Now, back to the quokka question," I said.

"I've devoted my life to the study of quokkas," Oscar declared. "It's no exaggeration to say I'm the world authority on *Setonix brachyurus*. Indeed, I'm scheduled to deliver the keynote address titled 'The Quokka Question' at the Global Marsupial Symposium next week."

"Global Marsupial Symposium?" said Ariana.

"You haven't heard of the GMS?" He sounded astonished. "Largely because of my sister's efforts, UCLA is hosting the symposium this year. It's arguably the most prestigious meeting of marsupial experts in the entire scientific world."

"Your sister?" said Ariana. "That wouldn't be Dr. Penelope Braithwaite, would it?"

"That's the one: Dr. Penny. She's more famous than I'll ever be." Oscar sounded disgruntled.

Ariana grinned. "I guess she is, but that's what you get when you're an expert on sex."

"Too true." He sighed. "I'm staying with Penny in her West Hollywood apartment. She can hardly walk out the door without someone recognizing her and coming over to badger her. And the questions they ask …"

I was lost. "Sorry, but I don't know who your sister is."

Oscar grunted. "Sometimes I don't either. On one hand she's Dr. Penelope Braithwaite of UCLA, noted expert on animal sexuality. On the other, she's Dr. Penny of talk radio—an odious program where people ring in with their grubby little sexual problems. I've told her a thousand times it's a prostitution of her talents—not that she ever listens to me."

He bent his shaggy head, apparently overcome in gloom.

"You said you thought you'd need a private investigator when you came to L.A. Why is that?" I asked.

"Professor Jack Yarrow," he spat out. His loathing plain, he went on,

"Yarrow claims that he is the world authority on quokkas. An American an authority on quokkas? Not bloody likely!"

"An academic rival?"

"A confidence trickster, who'd got to where he is by stealing other people's work and passing it off as his own. The pity is that an institution of the caliber of UCLA would have a charlatan like Yarrow on staff." He shook his head.

Using my advanced detecting skills, I said, "And I reckon this Professor Yarrow is appearing at the Global Marsupial Symposium too."

"He is," Oscar ground out. "But that's not the worst of it. Just before I left Australia, Penny called me to say she'd heard on the academic grapevine that the bastard is going to get up at the symposium when I begin my keynote address and publicly accuse me of plagiarizing his work on quokkas."

Oscar thumped himself hard on the chest. "Accuse me! When the truth is, Yarrow has plundered my research!"

"Have you any proof of this?" Ariana asked.

"I have my suspicions," he said darkly. "I believe one of my graduate assistants, Erin Fogarty, copied essential areas of my life's work and sold it to Yarrow." Oscar shook his head again. "Academic betrayal is the greatest betrayal of all. Frankly, I'm heartbroken."

"Why do you think Erin Fogarty's involved?" I asked.

His shoulders slumped. I wondered if he'd had a personal interest in this sheila. "Suddenly, last month," he said, "Erin left the quokka project. She said she'd unexpectedly inherited money and was continuing her studies in America."

I jumped as Oscar whacked my desk with his fist. "And what do you think I find when I get to Los Angeles, eh?" He turned his head to Ariana, then to me, and back again.

I was happy to take a stab at an answer. "Erin's working for Professor Jack Yarrow?"

"Yes!" My desk vibrated to another hearty whack. "Professor-bloody-Jack-bloody-Yarrow!"

"What do you want Kendall & Creeling to do for you?" asked

Ariana.

Her cool tone seemed to calm him. "Discredit Yarrow," he said. "Show him up for the fraud he is." He swung his attention to me. "I've set it up for you, Kylie. My sister can get you into UCLA as a visiting graduate student. You can take it from there, but be very careful. Jack Yarrow is a dangerous man."

Crikey, he had more confidence in me than was justified. "I've never been to university," I pointed out.

"Kylie can carry it off," said Ariana with assurance.

I shot her a look. Did she mean it? Apparently, she did, as she gave me a small, warming smile.

For the next few minutes we discussed the logistics of inserting me into UCLA as a student, Kendall & Creeling fees, and our reporting protocol for clients.

When our meeting concluded, Oscar Braithwaite got to his feet. I asked if I could get him a taxi, but he said that he was looking forward to getting out in the fresh air and would enjoy the long walk back to West Hollywood. I reckoned he'd be pushing it to find much fresh air on Sunset Boulevard, but he'd soon find that out for himself.

After we'd all ceremonially shaken hands again, Oscar retrieved a rather crumpled white envelope from the inside pocket of his suit coat. "Don't open this unless something happens to me. My sister has a copy too."

"You fear for your safety?" Ariana asked as he handed the envelope to me.

"I don't want to sound melodramatic," Oscar said in a serious low-key manner, "but Jack Yarrow is in my estimation a sociopath. He's capable of anything."

Ariana was leaving for an appointment in the Valley, so she saw Oscar Braithwaite out. I got busy at my computer, tapping in all the details of the meeting while they were fresh in my mind. It occurred to me that I hadn't found out what the question about quokkas was. I made a mental note to ask Oscar next time I saw him.

I'd just got to the pleasing point where I'd labeled a folder BRAITHWAITE, OSCAR when I heard the sharp *dot! dot! dot!* of someone running

5

down the tiled hallway in high heels. It had to be Melodie, Kendall & Creeling's receptionist and aspiring actress.

She burst through the door, blond hair flying, green eyes wide. "Kylie! Come quick! That guy who was just here—he's been run down by a car on Sunset Boulevard!"

TWO

I flew out the front door and galloped down the street to the scene of the accident. An ambulance had already arrived, and a police car, lights flashing, was parked half on the footpath. The traffic was treacling by, as motorists slowed down to get a look. Even though it was still pretty early in the morning, a large mob had formed, mostly made up of tourists—I knew this from the cameras slung around their necks. Everyone was pressing forward to enjoy the show, not at all discouraged by a young cop in uniform, whose perspiring face was flushed as he tried in vain to keep order.

Pushing my way through the throng was hard work. Good thing I'm tough; otherwise, I'd have had a cracked rib from the elbows that jabbed me on the way. I made it to the front to find two blokes in white trying to get their very uncooperative patient—Oscar Braithwaite throwing a wobbly—onto a gurney. Many cameras—digital and video—were trained on the action.

"What happened?" I said to the person next to me, an ancient woman wearing a dusty cloche hat pulled down over her eyebrows. No camera, so she was not a tourist.

"Hit-and-run," she said, not taking her avid stare from the altercation in front of her. "SUV. Big'un. SOB didn't stop. They never do."

"They're shooting a movie," someone said behind me. "That's Robin Williams under all that hair."

"No! Robin Williams?" The name ran through the rapidly expanding audience like wildfire. People passing stopped until the crowd got big enough to spill onto the roadway. Indignant horns added to the clatter of a helicopter overhead.

I did my best to get to Oscar, but the young cop got in the way. "I know him," I said. "He's my client." But the cop was occupied with crowd control and didn't listen.

Struggling mightily, Oscar Braithwaite shouted, "You're not taking me to bloody hospital! It's too bloody expensive!"

Many in the crowd murmured in agreement. "Health care in this country is capitalism gone mad, raping the working man," declared one scruffy bloke.

"And woman," snapped an angular sheila in bright pink pants. "You men always forget the women."

Someone clapped. That got a laugh.

"Let me go!" Oscar managed to free himself from his would-be rescuers. "I'm not bloody hurt. Just a few bumps and scratches." He spread his arms and wiggled his fingers. "Look. Nothing's broken."

"My kids love Robin Williams," someone said. "He's so funny. They've nearly worn out the DVD of *Mrs. Doubtfire*."

"His last picture bombed. Box office poison."

"That's not Robin Williams," declared someone else. "It's Jim Carrey."

That got a reaction. Cameras clicked anew; people surged forward; the cop, overwhelmed, headed for his patrol car, no doubt to call for backup.

"Jim! Jim! Look this way!" shouted a fan.

"I love Jim Carrey," remarked someone else. "He's so funny!"

"Can't do serious, though. His last serious picture bombed."

A spherical woman in a purple-and-orange muumuu hustled her equally globular kid to the front of the crowd. "Go on, Donnie. Ask Mr. Carrey for his autograph."

"Don't wanna."

"Yes, you do, you little creep," she hissed.

"Don't."

Oscar snatched the book and pen from the scowling kid and scribbled something down. Triumphant, the woman peered at the page. She frowned. "Oscar who?" She glared accusingly at him. "Why are you pretending to be Jim Carrey?"

The crowd murmured, not pleased. I raised my voice to say, "He's not pretending to be anybody. He's a dinky-di Aussie just visiting Los Angeles."

"It's identity theft," someone called out. The crowd growled.

"Oscar," I said, indicating the ambulance blokes, who were standing with arms folded and looking browned off, "you'd best go with them. The crowd's turning ugly. I'll get my car and follow along and meet you at the hospital."

"Bugger that," said Oscar, truculent.

"Arrest him," demanded the muumuu mother to the cop who'd returned to the scene. "He's impersonating a film star."

"Stuff it!" Oscar clambered onto the gurney. "OK, mates, you win. Bloody take me to the bloody hospital."

There was a dangerous rumble from the crowd as the gurney bearing Oscar was shoved into the back of the ambulance. "Don't let him get away!" someone yelled.

Yerks! Time for diversionary tactics. "That's not a cop," I shouted. "It's Brad Pitt!"

Pandemonium.

Oscar Braithwaite had put on a real performance in the hospital emergency. I hadn't liked hanging around there for hours any more than he did, but there was no need for him to yell at the nurses that way. By the time he was released—he had a few scrapes and bruises, but I reckoned all that hair had acted like a buffer—I was having second thoughts about my client. He was showing all the signs of being a yobbo of the first order.

I told myself maybe I was being a bit hard on the bloke, as he'd had a pretty harrowing experience. The way Oscar told it, he'd been standing on the curb with a bunch of other people waiting for the lights to change so he could cross Sunset Boulevard, when someone had given him a tremendous shove, right between the shoulder blades. He'd been rocketed out into the traffic, bounced off a humongous SUV, narrowly missed going under the wheels of a bus, and ended up in the gutter, knocked half silly.

"Bloody-Jack-bloody-Yarrow," he snarled. "He's behind it. If he didn't try to murder me himself, he got someone to do it for him."

Attempted murder? I suggested Oscar take his suspicions to the cops quick smart. That got him shaking his shaggy head violently. No way was he getting the law involved, he said, as that would just play into Jack Yarrow's hands. Yarrow would brand him as a total ratbag, a weirdo making wild accusations.

The doctor who examined Oscar wanted to admit him to the hospital for observation overnight, but Oscar started bellowing about how he'd spoken to his sister and how she'd dipped out of a faculty meeting at UCLA just so she'd be home to look after him. "Kylie here can drive me to Pen's place as soon as you bloody let me go."

By the time I got Oscar into my new car—I'd collected it just two days earlier—he'd worn himself out with all that yelling. He settled into the front seat, a bad-tempered hairy bundle.

My new vehicle was a dark-gray Toyota Camry. It was nice enough but rather boring. It wasn't half the fun to drive as my dad's restored red Mustang but much more suitable for surveillance operations, where I was supposed to blend in with the traffic. Not that I'd done any proper surveillance yet, but I'd practiced a few times. I had to admit I needed to polish my skills a bit in that area. One bloke I'd picked out to follow had pointed me out to a motorcycle cop, and I'd had to talk fast to get out of hot water.

Oscar gave me his sister's address, and I checked the location in *The Thomas Guide*. This took a bit of time, as the directory seemed to have a zillion streets, many with the same name. Los Angeles was just too big for any one person to know all of it well. My hometown, Wollegudgerie, would have fitted into one of L.A.'s suburbs a couple of times, with plenty of space left over.

"There's a fair chance I'll get lost," I said.

Oscar grunted and closed his eyes.

We set off into the heavy afternoon traffic, and I quite pleased myself by finding Dr. Penelope Braithwaite's street with only one little detour in the wrong direction. Oscar didn't even notice this small blip, as he was slumped in his seat, now and then mumbling "Bloody

Yarrow" to himself.

When I drew up in front of his sister's apartment block, by extraordinary good fortune snaffling a vacant parking spot, Oscar roused himself to say, "Come on up and meet Pen. You need to discuss how she's getting you into the biology department at UCLA."

Dr. Penelope Braithwaite snatched open the door of her apartment before Oscar could turn his key in the lock. "Oscar, you silly bastard, what have you been doing to yourself?"

This sheila certainly made an instant impression. She was oversize in every way, being both taller and wider than me, and possessing a loud, confident voice whose ringing tone I reckoned could be heard out in the street. Her hair sprang from her scalp in tawny waves, cascading down to her broad shoulders. Her face had definite features—huge, lustrous gray eyes; an emphatic nose; a wide, full-lipped red mouth. I caught a glimpse of large, square teeth, which were very white .

"It was Yarrow," Oscar ground out.

"Oh, Yarrow," she said dismissively, waving us both in. She shook my hand with a grip just short of painful. "You must be Kylie Kendall, my brother's private eye."

"G'day, Dr. Braithwaite," I said, wondering if I should set her straight about my trainee status.

"Shove the doctor bit," she said, flashing her teeth in a big smile. "Call me Pen."

"Right-oh."

"I suppose you've already discovered that my brother's a bit of a whinger."

'Strewth, this was a trifle heartless. The bloke had nearly been killed. "Your brother did say he was deliberately shoved into the traffic."

She raised her eyebrows. They were significant, like the rest of her. "Yeah?" Turning to him, she said, "You really think Jack Yarrow tried to kill you? If so, he's obviously managed to clone himself, since from early this morning he's been in the same long, boring meeting I've had to endure."

"Then he paid someone to do it."

Penelope put her hands on her hips. "Listen up, bro. You spend your

11

life tramping around the bush, taking your own sweet time about things. People in this town are notoriously impatient. Someone at the back of the pack pushes the guy in front of him, who pushes whoever's in front of him, and voilà!—you end up on the roadway."

Oscar jutted out his lower lip. "It was deliberate. If it wasn't bloody Jack Yarrow, it was someone working for him." He shook his head emphatically. "Attempted murder, that's what it was."

She gusted a large sigh. "And what do you propose to do about it? Call the cops?"

Oscar jerked his head in my direction. "No need. Kylie here's already on the case."

"I am?"

Crikey, I had a suspicion I'd have my hands full trying to impersonate a graduate student and getting the goods on Professor Yarrow about the plagiarism. Adding attempted murder to the mix was a bit much.

"There's a problem?" Penelope Braithwaite said, towering over me. She'd have been a ripper basketball player.

"I have to consult with my partner."

"Fair enough," she conceded. "We'll have to negotiate a larger fee to cover extra services."

"But you don't think your brother was deliberately pushed," I pointed out.

She gave him an indulgent look. "He's a boofhead, of course, but if it'll set his mind at rest, it's worth the money."

Hell's bells! This case was getting complicated. "I'll get back to you," I said.

THREE

It was mid afternoon by the time I made it back to Kendall & Creeling. I was absolutely starving, having skipped lunch. I barged through the front door and up to the reception desk, which was empty. This was where Melodie should be—if she hadn't ducked out on one of her many auditions. In theory Melodie was supposed to man the phone in office hours, except for lunchtime, when Fran took over for her. Since Melodie's recent run-in with my business partner Ariana over her many absences, Melodie had promised to try to restrict her auditions to lunchtime or after work—try being the operative word.

The phone rang. I was about to answer it myself when Lonnie appeared, wandering down the hall eating a pastry. He hastily swallowed a mouthful, seized the phone, and said without much enthusiasm, "Kendall & Creeling."

The call dispatched to Bob Verritt, Lonnie gave me a glum look. He was usually the happy sort, flashing his little-boy dimpled smile, but right now he was clearly feeling low.

"Don't ask," he said, then when I didn't, he added moodily, "I can't believe I fell for one of Melodie's heartrending audition stories."

"You swore the other day you'd never fall for one again."

Lonnie shook his head, so that a lock of floppy brown hair fell over one eye. "And I meant it. But she's good, Kylie. I was saying, 'No way, José' one minute, and 'Break a leg' the next."

I knew "break a leg" was a traditional show-business good luck wish, but considering the height of Melodie's high heels, perhaps unwise. "When will she be back?"

Lonnie blew out his lips in an exaggerated sigh. "She said an hour or so. I'm figuring two, at least. So I'm stuck here answering the phone. He gave me a speculative look. "Kylie, you wouldn't—"

"No way, José!"

Lonnie's shoulders drooped. "Harriet turned me down too. Bob just laughed, and Fran…" He rolled his eyes. "Well, you know Fran."

I did indeed know Fran. She and I were very often at daggers drawn. "Fran said no?"

"Fran offered to rip me a new one." He brightened up to say, "There's a message for you from your Aunt Millie."

A wave of foreboding swept over me. "She's not coming back to L.A. is she?"

"Unfortunately, she's not," said Lonnie, grinning. He knew very well the trouble I'd had with my Aunt Millie when she'd lobbed over from Wollegudgerie to persuade me to go home to Australia and help run Mum's pub. "She says she's done New York. Now she's on her way to London on a round-the-world trip."

My spirits lifted immediately. "You beaut! That's bonzer news."

Lonnie's smile widened. "But she says she had such a great time here, she coming back real soon."

My spirits sank. "How soon?"

"She didn't say."

This was not good. I took myself off to the kitchen for comfort food—a peanut butter sandwich and a good strong cup of tea. Julia Roberts stalked in while I was spooning Twining's Ceylon Orange Pekoe into the teapot. She watched me for a moment, then gave a single plaintive meow to indicate her near starvation.

"Jules, you had breakfast not that long ago."

A look of deep displeasure appeared on Julia Roberts's tawny face. She hated to be crossed.

"Oh, all right," I said, looking in the cupboard for her prawn-and-tuna treats. I only put six into her bowl, not wanting to ruin her appetite for dinner. Jules inspected the six closely, gave me a triumphant wiggle of her whiskers, and walked off, leaving the bites untouched. Score one to Julia Roberts, nil to Kylie Kendall.

I took my tea and sandwich back to my office and sat down to go through the accounts. As part owner of Kendall & Creeling, I took an interest in the day-to-day running of the place. Back in Australia, I'd handled all that side for Mum's pub, Wollegudgerie's Wombat's Retreat, so I knew my way around anything financial. This last month I'd noticed a big jump in the amount spent on office supplies, so I started to go through the invoices to find out why.

"Blimey," I said, coming upon an invoice for forty one-gallon plastic containers of water. *What is that for?* And the next invoice raised my eyebrows even higher: yards of heavy plastic sheeting plus fifteen rolls of duct tape.

Time to find Fran. She'd bestowed on herself the title office manager and had taken it as one of her duties to handle most of the ordering, so she was the one to explain why we needed these large quantities of water, plastic sheeting, and tape.

There was still no Melodie to be seen, and Lonnie had disappeared, but Fran was standing at the front desk, arms folded. She was smiling as she surveyed a large pile of boxes. It was always a surprise how pretty she was when not surly.

Standing beside Fran, my least-favorite delivery bloke in the world was surreptitiously surveying her cleavage. This wasn't surprising, as Fran had a spectacular bust line that was shown off to advantage with a tight scarlet top that rather clashed with her red hair.

"I'd like nothing better than to help you out," the delivery bloke was saying, "but my job description says I deliver goods inside the front door. Not one inch more."

Fran's smile vanished as though it had never existed, and her customary scowl darkened her face. "What? After all the business we give your company, you can't meet a simple request?"

"Look at it from my point of view. Moving this stuff to your storage room is above and beyond—"

He broke off as he saw me, and a nasty smile appeared on his face. "And how's the trainee gumshoe today? Putting the wind up the bad boys?"

This bloke was just a smart aleck in a yucky brown uniform who thought I was fair game for a bit of chiacking ever since he'd caught me studying *Private Investigation: The Complete Handbook.*

"Rip-snorting," I said.

"Rip-snorting?" He chortled suggestively. "What're you saying? That you Aussie chicks are hot stuff?"

"Dream on," said Fran. "Rip-snorting means excellent." When I looked at her, surprised, she added, "I'm good at obscure foreign languages."

Of course she was having a go at me, but I didn't rise to the bait. "When you've got a free minute," I said, "I'd like to go over some invoices with you."

Fran's dark expression got distinctly darker. "And which particular invoices would those be?"

"Why did you order forty gallons of water?"

"Disaster supplies."

"Forty gallons?"

Fran was like Julia Roberts—she didn't take kindly to being crossed. "Yes, forty gallons," she said in a cold tone, "and that may not be enough."

"Enough for what?"

There was a pause while Fran decided whether or not to fill me in. At last she said, "Each person needs at least one gallon of water per day for drinking and sanitation purposes."

The delivery bloke, who'd been listening closely, sniggered. Hooking his thumb in the direction of the boxes he'd delivered, he said, "If you want disaster supplies, you've got 'em right here. Military food rations, battleground medical kits, disposable face masks, sleeping bags…"

"You're setting up an army hospital?" I inquired of Fran.

"Oh, go ahead and joke, but a cataclysmic event could occur at any moment," she snapped. "For example, take a terrorist attack. It could be nerve gas, smallpox, or anthrax, or radiation from dirty bombs, sabotage of food and water—the list goes on. And that's not to mention natural disasters—earthquake, flood, fire, volcanic activity, tsunamis, meteor strikes, tornadoes. Victims who don't die in the first few seconds often linger on to suffer dreadfully."

She looked quite chuffed at this last statement. Fran really did enjoy the gloomy side of life. "Suffer dreadfully," she repeated. "Beg for death."

Even the delivery bloke looked a bit taken aback. "It all sounds pretty hopeless, doesn't it?" he said.

"It's un-American to be hopeless," Fran declared, not impressed with his attitude. "Homeland Security asks every citizen to be optimistic, but at the same time be fully prepared for the worst. That's what I'm doing. Being optimistic about the future, but preparing for disaster."

I managed not to remark that optimism was the last quality Fran could claim. "You're storing all this stuff in the room next to mine?" I asked.

"That a problem?" Fran's tone indicated it better not be. "It is the office storage room."

I had had plans for that particular area, at the moment full of office supplies. My accommodations in the Kendall & Creeling building had a grand total of two rooms: a bedroom with bathroom attached. This adjacent storage area would make a wonderful sitting room, once I had a door installed in the dividing wall.

Obviously not interested in whether it was a prob for me or not, Fran was off and running. "Apart from ordering emergency supplies," she said, "as office manager, it's my responsibility to bring everyone up to speed as far as disaster is concerned. Later today I'll be putting up easy-to-read diagrams clearly showing escape routes from the building in the event of a catastrophe."

"Bit of a waste of time," I said, "as there's not much choice. Like, you go out the front door, or you go out the back door. And they've both already got illuminated exit signs. I reckon we don't need a diagram."

Fran's eyes narrowed to slits. Opposition didn't sit well with her.

"I'm out the front door," said the delivery bloke hastily. He'd seen Fran on the warpath before.

She watched him leave, then turned to me. "Coming from the center of Australia, like you do, you can't be expected to appreciate the terrorist situation in the way an American would."

"Oh, I think I could have a lash at it. Empathy's my strong suit."

"You don't have a clue."

"I may have a ghost of an inkling," I said cheerfully.

I wondered how Fran would go if she were dropped in the harsh Outback. I was sure I could live off the land and survive. I was guessing Fran wouldn't be so lucky, though when I thought about it, she really was one tough sheila. I could imagine her running down a kangaroo and dispatching it with her bare hands.

"What are you thinking about?" Fran asked, glaring at me suspiciously.

"I was wondering about the plastic sheeting and duct tape."

Fran assumed an I'll-tell-you-but-you'll-never-get-it expression. "In a terrorist attack, you need to protect yourself from germ warfare and deadly gases by sealing off all entry points. We'll use the plastic sheeting and duct tape to close everything off. And, as an added precaution, we'll all wear face masks."

"What about Julia Roberts?"

Fran gave me a sour smile. "If you can fit Julia Roberts with a face mask, good luck."

I gave the scenario a bit of thought. "If everything's sealed off, won't we all suffocate?"

Fran clicked her tongue in irritation. "Eventually, if we stay here long enough, but our battery-powered radios will tell us when it's safe to go outside."

"What if it never gets safe?"

Totally fed up with me, Fran snarled, "Then we die, Kylie. We all die a horrible death."

FOUR

I was waiting impatiently for Ariana to come back from her appointment in the Valley so I could discuss the developments in the Braithwaite case. Ariana was involved in a detailed security analysis for a furniture company's warehouse, and that would take most of the day, so I knew she might not even bother returning to the office. Still, I could hope.

Half an hour or so was spent writing a letter to Mum. I'd have much preferred to e-mail her, but Mum said reading on a computer screen was too impersonal. She wanted handwritten communications. Fair enough, but I knew she had an ulterior motive. Mum fancied herself a handwriting analyst, having just completed the course "Handwriting: The Hidden Revealed" in an adult education course held at Wollegudgerie High on weekday evenings. She'd confided to me she'd been quite shocked at what she'd learned from the signatures of various apparently law-abiding guests staying at the pub.

I suspected Mum would be studying my writing for evidence I was holding out on her and not being entirely open about what was happening here in the States. Fair dinkum, I wasn't keeping anything back, but hell's bells, I was tempted at times.

She'd had made me promise to keep her totally up-to-date on my new career. I knew very well my mum was hoping I'd make a proper mess of private-eyeing, and lose interest in staying here in L.A. Pity about that, since I was absolutely determined to become a crash-hot private detective. Besides, there was Ariana Creeling.

Blond, blue-eyed, self-contained Ariana Creeling. I could visualize her down to the smallest detail, slim and supercool in her customary black. To be realistic, I'd probably never had a ghost of a chance with Ariana, being close to her total opposite, not just in looks but in personality and background.

The fact that I wasn't thin and had brown eyes, boring brown hair, and olive skin didn't really matter, I suppose. And maybe my coming from a little town in the Outback of Oz wasn't an insurmountable barrier. What did matter was my tendency to be impulsive, to open my mouth before my brain was in gear. No one would call me detached; quite a few would call me a galah.

I'd already pretty well blown it with Ariana by blurting out that I adored her, just when I'd promised myself the only way to behave was to be offhand and megacasual, and wait for the faint possibility she'd come my way.

Oh, I knew at heart it had never been likely she'd fall in love with me, but as my mum always says, nothing ventured, nothing gained. So I was venturing, in a tentative sort of way, and hoping against hope to gain something. A warm friendship would do. Crikey, I was kidding myself again. I wanted something much more incendiary from Ariana.

I dragged my thoughts back to my letter to Mum. I dutifully told her all about Oscar Braithwaite and his brush with death, even though I knew when she read it she'd drop everything and rush to the phone. I knew exactly how the call would go. Mum would emphasize that it was only a matter of time until violence came my way, and I might not be as lucky as Oscar. She'd pause for a moment to let that sink in, then she'd demand I come home to Wollegudgerie before I was run down, or shot, or carjacked. Unfortunately, every lurid news item about Los Angeles seemed to make the television news in Oz, so my mum was convinced I was pretty well in danger twenty-four seven.

I folded the pages carefully and slid them into an envelope addressed to Mum at The Wombat's Retreat, Wollegudgerie. No street address was needed, as everyone in my hometown knew the location of the only pub. I printed AIRMAIL and underlined it several times, ditto AUSTRALIA.

I'd never quite got over the way the posties here collected mail as well as delivered it. Everyone in the States seemed to think this unremarkable, but where I came from, if you tried this on, the postie would give you the hairy eyeball and point you in the direction of the nearest red postbox.

The mail was delivered to Kendall & Creeling around midday, so I'd missed the collection. Melodie always took any late letters and posted them on her way home, so I trotted up to the front desk to see if she'd finally returned from her audition.

She had. "Did you see me in the Refulgent ad last night?" she asked the moment she saw me. "It was on several times."

This tooth-whitening commercial was Melodie's first real success in the acting business, so she was milking it for all it was worth.

"Didn't watch TV," I said, taking the easy way out.

"Prime time," Melodie announced with pride. "Network television. Larry-my-agent says it's wonderful exposure."

I'd heard Melodie refer to her agent this way so many times that in my head I always ran the words together.

"What does Larry-my-agent say about your movie voice-over?"

I was genuinely interested in a horrified sort of way, as Melodie was in the running to voice an Aussie character in an animated movie. Her attempt at an Australian accent would have any genuine Aussie howling with derision, but Melodie's voice coach kept assuring her it was spot on.

Suddenly aware that Melodie's body language had switched from elated to deepest gloom, I asked her sagging figure, "There's a prob?"

She shook her head despondently, her long blond hair flying around photogenically. It just wasn't fair the way she looked good, no matter what.

"The studio hasn't green-lighted the movie yet." A sigh. "And I've worked so hard on the Aussie accent. Malcolm, my voice coach, says Aussie's a terrific challenge. One in a thousand have the ear, you know. It's like having perfect pitch, my voice coach says."

I barely stopped myself from telling Melodie exactly what I thought of her voice coach, who clearly wouldn't recognize a genuine Australian accent if his life depended on it. Changing the subject to something safer, I said, "What happened to all the boxes that were here before?"

"The disaster stuff? Fran moved it. She wanted me to help carry the boxes to the store room, but I couldn't"—she flashed her fingers in my direction—"because I've just had my nails done and the polish is hardly dry. Like the color? It's new. My manicurist says it's the latest thing."

Melodie's nails were an odd sort of yellowish puce color. No way could I honestly admire them. Besides, technically she was my employee, and I was about to lower the boom. "Melodie, you promised, if you could, to schedule your auditions at lunch or after work," I said severely. "And I don't recall time for manicures was included."

Melodie blushed a little, but not much. "I knew Lonnie was looking after the phone, so…"

To her obvious relief, Bob Verritt, tall and scarecrow-thin, chose this moment to angle his way through the front door. He was juggling two big rectangular shapes wrapped in brown paper. I didn't need to ask what they were, and neither did Melodie.

"More old-movie posters?" she said with a touch of scorn. The walls in Bob's office were covered with framed posters from the decades Bob enthusiastically referred to as the golden age of film.

"*Bringing Up Baby* and *The Unforgiven*," he said, his homely face split in a grin. "Mint condition. Cost a fortune but worth every cent."

Melodie showed a degree of interest. "Did you say *The Unforgiven*? I just love Clint Eastwood. He's an actor's director, you know. I can see myself working with him in a small, intense, meaningful movie."

"You've got the wrong movie," said Bob, resting the weight of the frames on the front desk. His knowledge of film lore always impressed me. "You're thinking of the early nineties film, *Unforgiven*. I'm talking about *The Unforgiven*, shot in 1960. My opinion? One of the best westerns of all time. Directed by Huston, it stars Burt Lancaster, Audrey Hepburn, Audie—"

"Yeah, very interesting," interrupted Melodie, her wide green eyes glazing over fast. She rallied to ask, "Bob, did you see me in the Refulgent ad last night?"

"As a matter of fact, I did. You were great."

"Oh?" Melodie was exceedingly pleased. "How was I great, exactly?"

Bob seemed puzzled. "Well, every way, I suppose. Just great."

"But how great? I mean, was it my appearance, or my interpretation?"

Bob frowned. "Interpretation? You didn't say anything."

It was Melodie's turn to frown. It was a sore point with her that she'd auditioned for a speaking part in the tooth-whitening ad, but ended up with an inferior role with no dialogue.

Too late, Bob realized what he'd said. "Of course you didn't need to use words," he declared hastily. "Your smile said it all."

"Really?" said Melodie, mollified.

She'd opened her mouth to ask him how her smile said it all, but Bob made his escape, saying, "Sorry, gotta go. Have to get these up on the walls."

He passed Fran, who was striding down the hall toward us with purpose on her face. "Kylie, I've been looking for you."

"And here I am." I waited with apprehension. Fran rarely wanted to see me about anything good.

Fran put her hands on her hips—she did that a lot—and declared, "The storage room is totally inadequate. Simply not big enough. We need more space."

"Well, if you didn't have forty gallons of water…"

Fran made an impatient gesture. "Water is essential for our continuing survival. Besides, there are more crucial disaster supplies coming. I've ordered gas masks."

"Stone the crows!" I said with a laugh. "Next you'll be telling me we're getting isolation suits for everyone."

Fran jutted out her shapely jaw. "And you don't think that's a good idea?"

I looked at her, speechless. She was fair dinkum!

"Where are we going to put all this stuff?" asked Melodie.

Fran fixed me with a militant stare. "I'm thinking a dedicated disaster annex," she said.

Ɔ

"So Fran took it rather to heart when I said I couldn't agree to having an annex dedicated to disaster supplies constructed at the back of our building."

Ariana and I were sitting in Ariana's stark black-and-white office. She'd turned up just as everyone else was leaving, which was bonzer, because I was dying to tell her all about Oscar and his possible attempted murder.

Ariana's lips twitched. "I imagine Fran wasn't happy with your decision."

I visualized Fran's face when I'd put the kibosh on her plan. Her porcelain skin had turned tomato-red, and for a moment I'd had a real fear she'd blow a gasket and fall lifeless at my feet. "You could say that."

"So where's she going to put all these disaster supplies? Is there really no space in the storage room?"

"Not a sausage," I said. "Besides, I've got an idea for that room."

A wary expression crossed Ariana's face. She'd already seen me go to work, knocking down a wall and installing a laundry alcove off the kitchen. "What sort of idea?"

"Tell you later," I said, not wanting to bring up a topic that would mean finding somewhere else to put all those office supplies. "Fact is, Fran's going to come to you direct. She says even if I don't, you will see the value of a disaster annex."

"I'm on your side, Kylie, all the way."

That gave me a ridiculous thrill. If it was only true about everything…

Wrenching my attention back to the matter at hand, I said, "Fran is a bit of a sad sack, isn't she? A proper miseryguts."

Ariana shook her head. Her pale, sleek blond hair was pulled back tightly in a chignon, so there was none of Melodie's shampoo-commercial activity. "I blame Homeland Security," she said. "Fran always tends toward pessimism, and the colored alert levels have just made her worse."

"It beats me where she gets it from," I said. "I mean, your sister Janette's got what I'd call a sunny personality."

Fran's mother and Ariana's sister was quite a famous artist and was known only by her first name. Janette had a cheerful nature, though as I thought about it, she did paint some rather disturbing things. That could point to something pretty dark in the deep recesses of her mind.

Ariana raised her shoulders in a minimal who-knows shrug. I wished I could manage to convey as much as that so gracefully. I wished—

"Kylie?"

Oh, stone the crows! I was staring again, and I'd spoken to myself severely about that before. I said hurriedly, "Did you hear what happened to Oscar Braithwaite this morning, after he'd left our offices?"

"I ran into Melodie as she was leaving."

Enough said. Melodie was part of the receptionist network, and prided herself, as they all did, on being the first source of sensational information whenever possible.

I gave Ariana a detailed rundown on what had happened, and how I'd driven Oscar home and met his sister. As she always did, Ariana listened with close attention, her eyes on me the whole time. 'Strewth, it was uncanny how intensely blue they were. I wondered if the color would fade when she got really old, so there'd eventually only be a faint suggestion of the jolt a look from her could give. I'd like to be with her long enough to find out—

"As soon as possible," said Ariana.

"Sorry?"

"I said it would seem there's a lot to discuss with the Braithwaites, so we need a meeting as soon as possible. I'm free tomorrow morning."

"I'm on it," I said. "Can I use your phone?"

"Of course."

I've always had a head for figures, and I'd memorized Penelope Braithwaite's phone number without difficulty. She answered at the second ring: "Braithwaite."

"Dr. Braithwaite, it's Kylie Kendall."

"Pen. Call me 'Pen.'" Her voice came roaring down the line and bounced against my eardrum. I moved the receiver further away. "What can I do you for, Kylie?" Hoot of laughter. Ariana raised an eyebrow.

Pen Braithwaite certainly was cheerful, considering her brother had just had a brush with death. I said with a suitably serious tone, "My partner and I have been discussing a meeting with you both, maybe tomorrow morning."

"Done! Time?"

I offered to hold the meeting at her apartment, as by tomorrow Oscar would certainly be feeling even more bruised and stiff, but Pen brushed that aside with a brisk, "Nonsense. It'll do him good to get out and about." She added heartily, "And Oscar says your partner's a bit of all right. I've always had a weakness for blonds. I can't wait to see for myself."

"Right-oh," I said, conscious that Ariana could hear every word the woman was bellowing. "So that'll be nine o'clock, here at Kendall & Creeling."

"Can hardly wait!"

I had the uneasy feeling she really meant it.

FIVE

It was such a beautiful early-summer morning that Julia Roberts and I had breakfast out in the backyard, which I'd furnished with a redwood table complete with big dark-green umbrella, matching chairs, and a reclining lounge with green all-weather cushions. I sat at the table with my porridge and a pot of tea. Jules reclined on the lounge, keeping a lazy eye on the bird life cavorting in the three trees.

The birds had the choice of citrus—lemon and lime—or an ancient jacaranda, and they were bouncing around making a hell of a racket. I thought this might be because of Julia Roberts, and that they were shrieking the equivalent of "Cat! Cat!" Then I noticed a gathering of crows on the roof, each an untidy bunch of glistening black feathers topped by a smooth head with bright, intelligent eyes and a murderous beak.

Crows in Australia were known to eat the babies of smaller birds, and I reckoned they would do the same here in the States. The nesting season was still underway, so the avian alarm in the trees was well-founded.

"Crows!" I said to Julia Roberts, pointing to the fat, curved red tiles of the roof. "Go get 'em."

One crow wandered casually down to the edge of the gutter and peered over. Jules gave the big black bird a desultory glance, then favored me with a wide pink yawn. It was apparent crow-scaring was not high on her to-do list.

"Gorgeous morning," said Harriet Porter, coming out the back door with a mug of ghastly herbal tea in one hand. I knew what it was from the brightly colored BlissMoments tag dangling down one side. Honestly, I could never understand how anyone could drink herbal tea, but Harriet gave every evidence of enjoying the stuff.

She sat down opposite me. "Sure I can't get you a cup of herbal tea?" she said teasingly. "Chamomile is nice. Calms and refreshes."

"Oh, please," I said. Harriet grinned.

She was working part-time at Kendall & Creeling while she put herself through law school. Soon, Harriet would be working rather less, as her pregnancy was well advanced. Harriet was one of those women for whom pregnancy was a breeze. Her chestnut hair was glossy, her complexion clear. She glowed with good health and never seemed to have her equanimity disturbed by things that would rile me and send Fran into a total hissy fit.

"I hear you have a client whose sister happens to be Dr. Penny of radio fame," Harriet said.

I sat back. "How did you know that?"

"One guess."

"Melodie."

Harriet nodded. "Melodie's a dyed-in-the-wool fan. Says she listens to the show every chance she gets."

"You'd better give me the good oil." When a faint shadow marred Harriet's sunny expression, I added a quick translation. "She and her brother are coming here this morning for a meeting with me and Ariana, so any background will be a help. What I'm asking is, what do you know about Dr. Penny and her show?"

"*Sexuality Unchained* is on after ten, and it's wildly popular. People call in and Dr. Penny answers any and all questions on sexuality—explains, gives advice, refers callers to other resources, and so on. No area's taboo."

"Blimey," I said, "that's a pretty wide field."

Harriet took a sip of her herbal concoction. I wrinkled my nose. I could smell it clear across the table. "It is," she said, "but I've never heard her thrown by a question."

"You listen to the program?"

"Sometimes." She laughed. "Often, actually. Dr. Penny's very entertaining."

"Does she take the micky out of callers? Send them up?"

"Not at all," said Harriet. "Dr. Penny treats every person's question seriously, even when it's obviously a setup. She gets a few of those."

"I bet she does," I said, thinking of sniggering little kids—of all ages—daring each other to make it through the screening to get to air with some puerile question.

"Dr. Penny opens and closes each session of *Sexuality Unchained* with a statement that sex is her great passion," said Harriet. "She gives every evidence that it is."

"I met her yesterday," I said. "She's a large woman in every way. It could be a bit quelling to be the object of her desire."

Harriet chuckled. "Dr. Penny proclaims herself proudly bi-sexual. She hasn't taken a fancy to you, by any chance, has she?"

"I've reason to believe she prefers blonds."

Harriet and I looked at each other and grinned.

"Your meeting this morning should be quite interesting," said Harriet.

⊃

Melodie called me from the front desk to say Oscar and Pen Braithwaite had turned up early for their appointment. Oscar, his hair even wilder than yesterday—I was betting he hadn't even combed it— was complaining under his breath, and was obviously in some pain. His sister seemed oblivious to his distress.

When I got there to collect them, Melodie was beaming up at Pen Braithwaite. "You're Dr. Penny! I just love your program!"

Pen Braithwaite beamed back. "Excellent. Do you have any question you'd like me to answer on air?"

Melodie looked rather nonplussed. "About sex, you mean?"

Pen flung her arms wide. "About sexuality. About the whole magnificent sweep of humanity's most intimate relationships."

Melodie blinked. "I can't think of anything at the moment, Dr. Penny, but thank you for asking."

She looked faintly alarmed when Pen leaned over her to inquire, "Have you plumbed the depths of your full, sexual being? Realized the sensual self in all its glory?"

"Um…" said Melodie.

I broke in to ask Melodie to tell Ariana our clients had arrived, and then I led the Braithwaites down the hall to my office, Oscar shuffling and Pen striding as though on parade. On the way we passed Julia Roberts, who gave brother and sister the once-over, clearly came to the conclusion they had little to offer, and continued on her way.

My office had originally been my dad's, and I hadn't changed the furnishings. He hadn't been a gray man in person, but that was the color he'd chosen for the charcoal carpet and metal furniture. I'd jazzed the room up a little with a wall full of framed Australian wildlife photos, but otherwise it was as he'd left it.

"Nice," said Pen, making a beeline for the photos. "You take these? Yes? Professional standard—I'm impressed."

"I need coffee," said Oscar, lowering himself gingerly into a chair. "Strong black coffee with a lot of sugar."

His sister snorted. "Coffee! You'd be better off without that muck in your system, Oscar."

Yerks! Don't tell me I had another herbal tea addict on my hands. "We have BlissMoments herbal stuff," I said to her. "Would you like a cup?"

Deep loathing appeared on Pen's face. "More muck," she boomed. "What's wrong with honest-to-God tea, eh? That's what I drink. Black, no sugar, and certainly no artificial sweetener of any kind."

A woman after my own heart. "Be back in a mo," I said.

Zipping off to the kitchen, I found Harriet inspecting the contents of the refrigerator. "What's happened to the peach-and-mango tea," she asked plaintively.

She laughed at my mimed revulsion. "Chill it, Kylie. Life's too short to waste strong emotions on tea."

"Flavored tea."

Harriet asked me why I was wasting time in the kitchen, as Melodie had told her the famous Dr. Penny of radio fame was in my office.

When I said I was getting coffee and tea for Dr. Penny and her brother, Harriet offered to make it for me. Bonzer woman, Harriet!

Ariana was just opening my door when I galloped back from the kitchen. I followed her into the room. Pen Braithwaite swung around from the wall, where she'd been examining the photos, and said, "Ah! The Creeling of Kendall & Creeling, I presume."

Oscar struggled to his feet. "This is my sister Penelope Braithwaite."

Pen was looking narrowly at Ariana. "Have we met before?"

"I don't believe so."

Still obviously puzzled, Pen shook hands, then flung her considerable self into a chair. "You were a cop—an officer with the LAPD." She flashed big, very white teeth. "I do my homework, you see." A hoot of laughter. "That mainly means Googling. Amazing what you can find out when you Google."

Ariana's still face didn't change. "I was with the LAPD."

Ariana's cool tone would have got me off the topic fast, but Pen Braithwaite persisted. "Why did you leave the force?"

"For personal reasons." Before Pen could frame another question, Ariana continued, "Shall we discuss your brother's case?" Turning to Oscar, she said, "If an attempt to maim or kill you was made, this puts an entirely different complexion on the matter. I strongly urge you to report the attack to the authorities."

"There was a patrol cop there at the scene," said Oscar. "He was worse than useless, but he would have to report the incident, wouldn't he?"

"Did you tell the officer someone had pushed you into the traffic?"

"No chance to. I was too busy arguing with the bloody blokes who were trying to strong-arm me into the bloody ambulance. What do you call 'em here? Paramedics?"

"No cops," said Pen Braithwaite decisively. "Don't trust the wallopers. Never have."

I would have pointed out to Ariana that a walloper was a police officer, but she clearly got the picture. "Wallopers are out," she said without a ghost of a smile.

Pen was eyeing Ariana speculatively. "I've placed you," she said. "We have met before, once a long time ago."

"I'm sorry, I don't recall."

The atmosphere in the room had subtly changed. I looked at Ariana. Her face was pale. Her shoulders stiff. A niggle of apprehension tickled my stomach.

Pen Braithwaite frowned, then her expression lightened. "Of course," she said triumphantly, "Natalie Ives. That's the connection, isn't it?" Silence. Then Ariana said, each word an ice cube dropped into the room, "This is not a matter for discussion."

Fortunately, before things could become even more awkward, Harriet knocked on the door with the tea and coffee, and after she left the meeting resumed with no reference to what had gone before.

I tried to concentrate, but, crikey, my mind was a bunch of whirling thoughts. Who was Natalie Ives? And why was Ariana acting this way? Usually, she was cool and reserved, but this morning, after Pen's mention of the name, Ariana had become positively arctic.

つ

At the conclusion of the meeting I saw the Braithwaites out to Kendall & Creeling's parking area. Pen Braithwaite drove one of those little Mazda sports cars that look like toys. It was turquoise in color, and with her size, she seemed to wear the vehicle rather than sit in it. I politely waited until they left, Oscar glum, Pen waving a cheerful goodbye, then came back into the building wondering what to do about Ariana. Not sure what the best course of action might be, I lingered at the front desk, where Fran and Melodie were chatting.

"Ashlee's getting snap-on teeth," Melodie was saying to Fran.

"Snap-on teeth?" I said. "What is Ashlee—a vampire?"

"Funny," said Melodie, not amused.

"Whose teeth?" Fran asked. "Not Gwyneth's, I hope. Those big square ones would be too much for Ashlee's little mouth." She paused to reflect. "Ashlee's mean little mouth."

"She chose Halle Berry's," said Melodie. "I think it's a big mistake. Everyone's got Halle Berry's."

"You've lost me. What's this all about?"

"I'd have thought," said Melodie, quite kindly, "that after you've been in the States this long, Kylie, you'd have a better grasp of what's going on."

"Fair go," I said. "I've only been in L.A. a few months."

"Years could go by," Fran observed, "and I doubt Kylie would be any more on the ball than she is now."

Blimey! This sheila worked for me, but I wasn't getting what you'd call much respect. Being the majority owner of Kendall & Creeling, I could give Fran the order of the boot, no worries. But she was Ariana's niece, so firing her probably wasn't a realistic option.

"Nice one, Fran," I said warmly, popping into the Pollyanna persona I knew drove her to distraction. "Thank you so much for your helpful criticism. I do so value your opinion."

Fran winced. Supersweetness really got to her. It was a little victory, but I savored it.

"In this town you've got to have a million-dollar smile," said Melodie. "There's the hard way and an easy way to get it. Ashlee's taken the easy way: snap-on, snap-off celebrity teeth. Myself, I believe in veneers."

"What is it with you lot?" I asked. "You're all tooth-obsessed."

"Veneers are excellent," said Fran, "but pricey. Quip's just had his front ones replaced. Cost a cool two thou a tooth."

I looked at her, gobsmacked. "Two thousand dollars each tooth!"

"It's an investment, Kylie. Quip needs to present well when he's pitching a script."

I visualized Quip, Fran's husband. He was a top bloke, and tall and handsome with it. And his smile, as I recalled, was pretty close to perfect. I said so to Fran.

She looked pleased. I reckoned she really did love him, though what a sunny person like Quip saw in Fran the Morose completely beat me.

"Veneers only last ten years," said Melodie. She rummaged around in her voluminous makeup bag and found a compact. Snapping it open, she bared her teeth for close examination in the mirror. "I wonder if my veneers need replacing."

The three of us gave Melodie's mouth the once over. "Looks grouse to me," I said. They both looked at me. "That means good," I said. "Excellent fangs, Melodie."

I had pretty good teeth myself, but came by them naturally. Good choppers ran in the family.

"You know Bob's front tooth, the chipped one?" said Melodie.

"Bonding," said Fran. "A few hundred dollars, and he'd have a great smile."

"I like Bob's smile the way it is," I declared. Bob Verritt was one of my favorite people, and I wouldn't change a thing about him.

Melodie rolled her eyes. "It's presentation, Kylie."

Ariana appeared, briefcase in hand. She gave us all a curt nod. "I won't be back today," she said, and left.

"What's eating her?" Fran asked.

I shrugged, wishing I knew.

SIX

I went back to my office feeling mega-low. If this kept up, Fran would have competition in the morose stakes. I fired up my computer and punched in www.Google.com. Then I hesitated with my cursor on the GO button. It would be just a matter of punching in a name and asking the Internet search engine to scan a zillion references and come up with possibilities.

But it was sneaky somehow to go behind Ariana's back and try to find out who Natalie Ives was. Of course, for all I knew, typing in that particular name might give me thousands of hits, and how would I know which ones referred to the Natalie Ives who had something to do with Ariana?

Perhaps I shouldn't bother. We were friends, weren't we? Perhaps tomorrow Ariana would get it off her chest, feel free to tell me all about this woman.

I snorted at this fantasy. That particular scenario was as likely as looking up to find tiny pink pigs circling the room with wildly flapping wings.

A quick check showed no pigs, pink or otherwise.

One of my mum's favorite sayings echoed in my ears: "Never put off until tomorrow what you can do today." She usually paired this with "He who hesitates is lost." I paused, irresolute. Don't put it off. Just do it. But what would Ariana think of me if I said to her, "I Googled 'Natalie Ives' and now I know who she is"?

Another of my mum's bits of life advice seemed appropriate. I should look before I leaped. So I shouldn't do anything, just wait and see what happened. After all, if Ariana had wanted me to have that information, she'd have told me, wouldn't she? But then, what chance did she have to do that before she left?

What if I'd gone straight back to Ariana's office after seeing the Braithwaites out, instead of stopping at the front desk? Ariana might have said to me, "I suppose you're curious about Natalie Ives." I would have replied supercasually, "Maybe a little interested." And Ariana would have said...

I sighed. *Said what?* I told myself to get a grip. I was blowing this out of proportion. It could simply be that Ariana disliked personal questions, and that was why she'd given Pen Braithwaite the big freeze this morning.

Then I remembered Ariana's tight, white face and her icy voice when she said, "This is not a matter for discussion."

I shoved back my chair and stood up. I wasn't Googling "Natalie Ives" today. Tomorrow, maybe...

I paced around my office, then forced myself to sit down and type up my notes on the Braithwaite meeting for my files. I squinted at my scrawl, which was more indecipherable than usual, because I'd been thrown by Ariana's reaction to Pen Braithwaite. In fact, I'd again clean forgotten to ask Oscar what the quokka question was. This was annoying, because the question of what the quokka question might be kept popping into my mind at odd moments.

During the meeting with the Braithwaites this morning, I'd done most of the talking on the Kendall & Creeling side. Ariana had only interposed with an occasional question or comment. After we'd discussed the altered fee structure for the additional investigation of Oscar's dive into the traffic on Sunset Boulevard, we'd got down to nitty-gritty of just how I was going to be set up at UCLA as a visiting graduate student.

Dr. Penelope Braithwaite occupied the endowed chair of animal sexuality in the psychology department, which was part of the College of Letters and Sciences. The endowment had been bestowed by a reclusive multimillionaire who had developed an abiding interest in penguins while wintering in the Antarctic. He'd been particularly struck by their sexual behavior.

"Bang anything, penguins," Pen Braithwaite had declared with approval. "Randy little buggers. Many documented examples of gay male penguins bonding for life. Lesbian penguins too."

The Global Marsupial Symposium was being hosted by the biology department of the university. Pen had a good friend on the inside, a member of the biology faculty who despised Professor Jack Yarrow and would be delighted, Pen assured us, to do anything to discredit the man as long as it was vaguely legal.

At that point I'd said, "'Vaguely legal?'"

Pen had snorted with laughter. "Rube's a bit of a chicken heart, but he and I"—she winked meaningfully—"have what you'd call a close, very personal relationship." Another guffaw. "Get my drift?"

Dr. Rubin Wasinsky was willing to take me on in the role of a short-term graduate student visiting from the University of Western Australia. He would make sure I had access to anything necessary—another broad wink from Pen Braithwaite—and I'd automatically be granted a pass to the symposium sessions and various functions too.

At that point Pen had whipped out her phone, a tiny silver thing that was entirely lost in her big hand. She got Dr. Wasinsky on the line to set up a lunch date for the three of us later that day. "We'll meet at the Ackerman Student Union," she'd announced. "Food's cheap and not half bad."

I finished my notes, printed them out, and put them in the new file folder. Then my mind obstinately went back to Ariana and Natalie Ives. Had they been lovers? Were they still lovers? Or maybe there was bad blood between them and they hated each other? Could this Ives woman be someone Ariana had arrested while she was still a cop? Was black-mail involved?

I had to stop obsessing about this. I snatched up the phone and punched in Chantelle's number. She was a receptionist, so she answered right away. "Good morning! United Flair Agency. How may I direct your call?"

"You can direct it to yourself. It's me."

"Honey, I was about to call you. Would you believe, I've got tickets to the premiere of *Bloodblot Horror II*. It's tonight. Can you come?"

Working for a talent agency as Chantelle did, she got quite a few perks, including free tickets for movies and theater productions. I was fond of Chantelle—we had a beaut, no-strings relationship with quite a bit of recreational sex thrown in—so I was more than happy to spend time with her.

Chantelle's taste in movies, however, didn't entirely agree with mine. She was a horror girl, the gorier the better. When the screen was awash with blood, I'd squint with distress, but Chantelle would watch the action with rather alarming gusto.

Although I knew the images on the screen weren't real, and just out of the frame a movie crew had been standing around while each ghastly, blood-soaked scene had been shot, I always got sucked in and let myself be scared silly. And I'd have awful nightmares later. Tonight, however, it'd be the perfect way to occupy my attention and drive away any thoughts about Ariana and the mysterious Natalie Ives.

I'd seen all the prepublicity for this R-rated splatter movie. Word was, members of test audiences had thrown up or fainted, or both. "Does it matter that I haven't seen *Bloodblot Horror I*?" I inquired.

"Of course not," said Chantelle. "They have nothing to do with each other, apart from the title."

"So why is it called the second *Bloodblot*?"

"Hold, please." Chantelle disappeared to take another call. A few moments later she was back, answering my question as though we hadn't been interrupted. It was a skill I noted all good receptionists developed.

"Because the name is a franchise, Kylie. When the first one was a huge box office success, it was inevitable there'd be a sequel. Hold, please." The line went dead again. A moment later a click was followed by, "I guarantee there'll be *Bloodblot III, IV,* and *V,* if the audience holds up."

We made a time for Chantelle to pick me up that evening—she seemed curiously reluctant to have me drive—and I put down the receiver. Maybe I should call Ariana on her mobile—I mentally corrected myself—on her cell phone and ask, "Are you OK?"

That wasn't all that terrif an idea, I decided. She'd answer coolly that of course she was OK and why was I asking? There didn't seem to be any good reply to that question. I could say I was interested, or be really up-front and say I couldn't bear to see her upset. That'd go down like a lead balloon.

I'd just have to wait until tomorrow when Ariana came to work. In the meantime, I had the Braithwaite case to worry about. I reminded myself that my client, Oscar, might be in mortal peril, although I had to admit he was a bit of a whinger, and maybe had imagined an impatient push from a stranger was really an attempt on his life.

Lonnie, being our computer guy and expert in all things electronic, was researching Professor Jack Yarrow for me. I went along to his messy office to see how he was getting along with the task. Because of his severe allergy to cats, coupled with Julie Roberts penchant for his company, Lonnie kept his door closed. This was usually futile, as Jules considered the whole thing a game, and would lurk nearby, dashing in at any opportunity and heading straight for Lonnie's protesting body.

A quick check of the hallway showed no Julia Roberts in evidence, so I knocked on Lonnie's door, faux-Spanish dark wood with copper studs everywhere, and took the muffled response to mean I was to come in. I found Lonnie peering into a monitor, his fingers tapping a staccato rhythm on the keyboard. "Be with you in a minute," he said without looking away from the screen.

Experience had taught me Lonnie's minute might last quite a long time, so I occupied myself assessing the possibilities of his room. Every surface, including the floor, was covered with an assortment of electronics, folders, papers, coffee mugs, and general debris. The room itself was quite large, and I mentally gathered up most of the stuff on the floor and put it into a series of spacious, imaginary cupboards I visualized taking up one wall. On another wall, a long bench could be installed to hold most of the electronic gizmos, and this would allow Lonnie's computer desk to be moved, so that anyone entering didn't immediately trip over him.

A touch of furnishing excitement generated more ambitious thoughts. If I could find places for everything in the storage room, plus

Fran's disaster supplies, my dream of adding a sitting room to my accommodations could be realized. Floor-to-ceiling storage units in here might be the ticket…

"Why are you looking like that?" said Lonnie, pushing off from the desk so his battered office chair swung him round to face me. There was dire suspicion on his face.

"Looking like what?"

"Like you've got plans for this room."

I said vaguely, "Plans?"

Lonnie flipped back the lock of limp brown hair that usually fell fetchingly over one eye to give him a cute little-boy appearance. "I thought we agreed my room was off-limits."

"We did?"

He used his dimples to advantage. "Come on, Kylie," he said persuasively, "you know I can't work in anything but this organized chaos. Besides, it's excellent security—no one but me can find anything." He made a sudden dive at a pile of manila folders on the floor, seized one and thrust one into my hands. "See! You wouldn't know to look for info on this Jack Yarrow guy down there, but I did."

My vision of storage cupboards shimmered, then disappeared. Lonnie could be awfully stubborn. I might be biting off more than I could chew here. It was a shortcoming of mine Mum had pointed out countless times. "Let's discuss it later," I said.

Lonnie swung himself back to his computer. "Let's never discuss it."

ɔ

Back in my office, I gave the Yarrow folder a quick flick-through, then checked my watch. I wanted to arrive at the UCLA campus early so that I could have a good look around and establish the lay of the land. I opened my copy of *The Thomas Guide* for Los Angeles County.

This street directory had been my salvation more than once. Each weekend, I'd ventured out alone, often driving Dad's red Mustang, to familiarize myself with freeways and surface streets. Each excursion, I'd managed to get more or less lost. But, I assured myself, I was getting better, although last weekend I'd found myself in the wilds of Chatsworth, and taken hours to find the way home. And even then I wasn't quite sure how I did it.

After much narrow-eyed study, I thought I had the route mapped out. Pen had advised me to dress like a student, so I changed into jeans, sneakers and a T-shirt with a koala on the front waving a flag that said: LAND OF OZ, tucked *The Thomas Guide* under one arm, and headed for the front desk to tell Melodie I'd be out until mid-afternoon.

She was on the phone. "And, Chloe, you'll never guess!" Melodie was saying, "Dr. Penny herself—What? Yes, that Dr. Penny. Anyway, she was real interested in me—What?" Melodie giggled. "Not interested that way, though she did ask me about my sex life—oh, hold on, I've got another call. Kendall & Creeling—Ashlee! You'll never guess who was here this morning—Dr. Penny!"

I cleared my throat. Melodie glanced back over her shoulder. "Ashlee? Gotta go. Call you back…. Chloe? Gotta go. Call you back."

"So Ashlee of the snap-on teeth is a receptionist," I said.

Melodie looked surprised. "How did you know?"

I didn't explain how now I always recognized the receptionist network in action. "Must be that I'm psychic," I said.

Melodie's surprise changed to keen interest. "Are you, Kylie? Me too."

"You're psychic?" I tried to hide my skepticism but obviously didn't do a crash-hot job, since an expression of deep hurt appeared on Melodie's face.

"Just because I never mention it doesn't mean I don't have the power. It's real personal, this sixth sense."

"How does this sixth sense manifest itself?"

Melodie looked at me distrustfully. I raised my eyebrows in an encouraging tell-me manner.

"Not that I see dead people or anything gruesome like that," she confided. "Mine's more in the premonition area. Knowing things ahead of time. For instance, I just knew the Refulgent commercial was to be mine. Somehow, I was aware through all the setbacks I endured, that it was my destiny to be a Refulgent girl."

Melodie paused to look at the ceiling, as though her inspiration was being beamed from above. "Sometimes I just creep myself out, when I have these flashes from the future."

"Crikey," I said, "this could be dynamite in the wrong hands."

"What could be?" said Lonnie, sauntering into view.

"Melodie's psychic powers."

Lonnie gave a great shout of laughter. This did not go down well with Melodie. "Oh, go ahead and laugh, Lonnie," she snapped, "but it's true that sometimes—often—I can see the future."

"It's called precognition," I added helpfully.

"OK, Melodie," said Lonnie in a challenging tone. "You go right ahead and predict something that will happen in my future." Before she could respond, he continued, "You can't, can you? 'Cause it's all bullshit."

Melodie shot out her lower lip in a pout. When I did this, I looked pathetic. Predictably, Melodie looked bonzer. "I can predict something in your future, Lonnie," she said. "Something that will definitely come true."

Lonnie folded his arms. "I'm waiting."

"Let me concentrate," said Melodie, closing her eyes and swaying a little in her chair.

"It's bullshit," said Lonnie to me.

"I see Julia Roberts," said Melodie, opening her eyes. "I see Julia Roberts greeting you in your office every morning."

Lonnie gave a cry of pain. "Not the cat!"

Melodie gazed heavenward as she intoned, "Sometimes Julia Roberts will be in your chair—sometimes she'll be hiding. But she'll be there, somewhere."

"You know I'm allergic," said Lonnie, a pleading note in his voice. "Melodie, you wouldn't do it to me, would you?"

"Ah, Lonnie," said Melodie with a brilliant smile, "you can't escape your destiny."

SEVEN

I had a rather shabby canvas backpack that I thought might be what a uni student would be likely to have. In it I put my cell phone, a pair of binoculars, a digital camera, and a miniature recorder Lonnie had given me. I intended to keep spoken notes of anything important I observed on the campus of the University of California, Los Angeles. That title was quite a mouthful, but it sounded so impressive. UCLA didn't have quite the same aura.

Fully prepared for the task ahead, I set off in my gray Camry with a feeling of confidence. *The Thomas Guide* made it clear that getting to UCLA was going to be child's play, even for a directory-challenged Aussie like me. All I had to do was head west on Sunset Boulevard toward the ocean. First I'd go through the Sunset Strip, a narrow canyon of billboards and buildings pressed close against the roadway. Night and day, crowds of sightseers filled the narrow footpaths, hoping to catch a glimpse of someone famous, or, failing that, to be somewhere where the famous had previously been.

Sunset Boulevard changed dramatically as it entered Beverly Hills. Here it became a broad road with a wide grassy strip down the middle. The buildings were imposing mansions set back from the traffic so that everything felt more spacious and less hurried.

I'd pass the famous pink bulk of the Beverly Hills Hotel on my right, then Sunset would take a series of sharp curves. I'd have to keep a lookout as soon as I entered Westwood, because I needed to turn left into Hilgard Avenue. At that point I'd be at the northeast corner of UCLA.

Everything went to plan, although I almost missed the signpost for Hilgard Avenue, and had to execute a left turn in haste, which was never wise, as left turns were a challenge for me. It was at moments like this that I tended to revert to driving on the other side of the road, as we did in Australia. Fortunately, this time I stayed on the correct side, and drove sedately down to the Westholme Avenue entrance of the campus.

Safely parked in Parking Structure 2, my one-day permit displayed prominently as required—the guy in the entrance booth had warned me that UCLA parking people were pitiless when it came to infringements of the rules—I set off to explore.

UCLA has a huge, beautiful campus, shaped rather like Australia's island state, Tasmania. Pen Braithwaite had given me a map with all the buildings marked, but she hadn't said how elegant many of them were, or how the landscaped grounds were full of trees and bushes, a lot of them Australian natives. I felt a pang of homesickness when I saw a spreading Morten Bay fig, its huge roots spreading out above the ground like gigantic claws hooking the tree into the earth.

The place was teeming with people of all ages and races. Most of them were walking in small groups, chattering like starlings, or talking with animation into phones. A few strode along alone, their intent expressions possibly showing they were contemplating some arcane scientific problem—or maybe the meaning of life in general. I'd given that one a bit of thought myself.

My jeans and T-shirt were the right choice, as I fitted right in. No one paid the slightest attention as I wandered along, snapping photos and recording any comments that came to mind. Actually, I felt a bit self-conscious recording myself. I never knew quite what tone to take. I was the only person who would hear my words, but I couldn't get the right breezy, informative quality. To myself, I always sounded like a dork.

There was a dynamic atmosphere at UCLA that lifted my spirits. Scaffolding here and there demonstrated that much building and refurbishing was going on, but it wasn't just that. The whole campus was alive with people thinking, things growing, changes to the world being made. I felt a pang that I hadn't gone to university myself. Maybe I could have made some difference, like so many of these students and faculty had, or were going to in the future. How would that feel, to be the first at something?

I sat down on a stone bench to consider what I might have studied, if I had gone on to higher education. I'd aced English at Wollegudgerie High, so maybe something in the literature line. Then there was the environment and ecology, because I loved everything to do with nature. Or perhaps something closer to hard science…

"Excuse me."

I looked up at a good-looking bloke who obviously knew how good-looking he was: black hair, good tan, soulful dark eyes. He gave me an oily smile. Perfect white teeth, naturally. "Are you alone?"

I cast a glance at the empty stone bench. "No," I said. "I have a row of invisible friends."

With one slick move he was sitting beside me. "A sense of humor, I like that. By the way, my name's Clifford Van Horden III, but those close to me"—pause to widen smile—"call me Cliff."

"G'day," I said. "I'll have to ask you to move. You're squashing one of my friends."

Cliff's smile wavered for a moment, then he chuckled. "Very funny. Love your accent. What is it? English?"

This was a mortal insult. English people hated being labeled Australian as much as Australians hated being labeled English. Something to do with the Aussies' convict background.

"If you don't mind," I said, "I'm from Oz."

Cliff's smile definitely sagged. I could see from his expression that he was wondering if his luck was bad, and he'd been trying to pick up a total drongo. He recovered to nod knowingly. *The Wizard of Oz,* of course. You're playing Judy Garland's character?" A guffaw. "You're not in Kansas anymore!"

I pointed to the koala on the front of my T-shirt. "Oz is the diminutive form of Australia," I said.

He examined my bosom. I had nowhere near Fran's breastworks, but what I did have Cliff seemed to appreciate. "So you're an Aussie, are you?"

Stone the crows, this bloke was dense. And he couldn't pronounce Aussie properly either. "It's *Auzzie*," I said.

"Great, great. But you haven't given me your name."

I checked my watch. Yerks, I had to get moving, or I'd be late for my lunch with Pen Braithwaite and Professor Wasinsky.

I got to my feet. "Sorry, Clifford Van Horden III," I said, "but I have to leave you."

"But I still don't know your name."

"Call me Judy," I said. "I'll leave it to you to guess the rest of it."

Ↄ

The Ackerman Union was full of noise—chattering people, clattering plates, music blaring. I followed instructions and found myself in front of a heated glass counter containing many pizzas, all looking mouthwateringly tasty. Mind you, they'd have to be good to equal Gino's Wollegudgerie Pizzeria.

When Pen Braithwaite had suggested meeting here, I'd asked if Professor Yarrow might see us together and later wonder why. She'd chortled at the suggestion. "Jack Yarrow be seen dead in a student union? Hah!" Apparently the chances were a snowball in hell's.

"Over here!" bellowed a familiar voice from a nearby table. Pen Braithwaite waved wildly. She'd pulled her hair back in a ponytail, but it seemed to have a life of its own, as many springy tendrils had escaped. She rather overwhelmed the man sitting beside her. He had a soft, cuddly body and wore a tattered brown cardigan. His face was long and amiable, reminding me of a particularly mild-mannered sheep.

"You've got to beat back the hordes around here to even get a sniff at a table," Pen declared, gesturing at the milling students. "Lunch is on me—no arguments. You and Rube hold the fort while I join the queue. Pizzas all round, eh?"

She marched off, then suddenly about-turned and marched right back. "You're not a vegetarian, are you?"

"Not lately."

"Good. Vegetarians are often quite odd. Perhaps you've noticed that." She marched off again.

"G'day, Dr. Wasinsky," I said. "I'm Kylie Kendall, your pretend graduate student."

Dr. Wasinsky shook my hand. His fingers were soft, but his grip was firm. "I go by Rube, no exceptions, even for respectful graduate students." His voice was light and melodious, and he sounded amused.

I slid onto an extremely heavy and uncomfortable metal chair. "Do you sing?" I asked.

He blinked his heavy-lidded eyes. "Why yes, in a choir. It's my secret vice."

"Tenor?"

"Indeed."

A burst of noise, overwhelming the general cacophony, erupted near the pizza area. Apparently an impatient student had been incautious enough to cut into the queue waiting to be served. Normally nothing much would have happened, I imagined, but this ferrety bloke had chosen Pen, perhaps thinking she wouldn't protest like someone younger would. Big mistake.

The ferrety student slunk off, Pen sent a triumphant look in our direction, and Rube said fondly, "She's a force of nature, Pen is."

"She is dynamic," I said diplomatically.

"Jack Yarrow hates her. He's a detestable individual, but I can hardly blame him. Pen takes every opportunity to mock the man, and Yarrow cannot abide being laughed at."

"No sense of humor?"

For a sheep, Rube suddenly looked quite fierce. "No sense of humor, no sense of honor, no sense of what's right and proper. That's why I was glad to offer my help. Yarrow's ridden roughshod over too many people. He deserves to be brought down a peg or two."

"If I can prove he plagiarized Oscar Braithwaite's quokka studies, what will happen to Professor Yarrow?"

Rube threw up his plump hands. "In a just world, it would impact negatively on Yarrow's reputation, but it isn't a just world, at least not in academia."

He leaned over the table, his expression severe. "You've heard of the recent accusations against respected historians? That they stole others' work and passed it off as their own?"

I vaguely recalled reading something about this, so I murmured "Hmm" encouragingly.

"So what happens?" Rube went on. "There's a brouhaha for a while. The academic in question wrings his hands and says lax attribution is the problem, not deliberate plagiarism—no, of course not!" He sat back in his chair, disgusted. "And Yarrow will brush it off the same way, and go on as before."

He brooded on this for a moment, then brightened to add, "But of course, his colleagues will know the truth. He'll be subtly damaged but damaged nonetheless."

"Pizza delivery!" Pen Braithwaite approached with a tray held high. She slapped down on the table a large plate absolutely loaded with pizza slices, then plunked down three red cans of Coke, paper serviettes and drinking straws. "Coke OK, Kylie? You don't go for the Diet stuff, do you?"

"Crikey, no. I drink Coke-Coke."

Pen whacked me on the shoulder hard. I'd check for a bruise later. "That's the ticket! None of that chemical muck." She sat down heavily, and snatched a slice of pizza. "Dig in, you two, or there'll be nothing left."

She wasn't kidding. The contents of the plate disappeared fast. Of course, Pen had a large body to fuel, but even so, I had to admire her ability to eat rapidly but quite neatly.

The last slice demolished, she sat back and grinned at me. Indicating Rube with a jerk of her head, she said, "What do you think of my man, eh?"

Rube got a bit pink. "Pen…"

"Dynamite," said Pen appreciatively. "And I'm an expert in the field."

Hell's bells! She had the expression of one about to fill in graphic details about her and Rube, details I was pretty sure I didn't want to hear. "About Professor Yarrow…" I said.

Pen's face darkened. "Bastard! If he did try to kill my brother, I'll have his guts for garters." She got to her feet. "Right, let's get to business.

I'll leave you two together to discuss the details. The sooner you get cracking, the sooner Yarrow bites the dust."

She strode off, with both of us looking after her. I glanced sideways at Rube Wasinsky. He wore a reminiscent smile. "Take my word for it," he said. "She's quite a woman."

⊃

The moment I opened Kendall & Creeling's front door, Melodie was on me. "Urgent message, Kylie. Your mom called while you were out. She's real upset."

I repressed a sigh. It was probably more problems with her fiancé, Jack O'Connell, who was dead set on running the whole show at Mum's pub, The Wombat's Retreat. He wasn't much chop at the financial side of things, so my mum was on a campaign to get me back home to straighten things out.

"OK, I'll call her back."

"It's winter in Australia," said Melodie with the air of one telling me something I didn't know, "but it's summer here."

"You had a talk with Mum about the seasons?" I was surprised, because my mother wasn't one for idle conversation.

Melodie looked virtuous. "Like, it was the least I could do to chat for a moment about the weather, seeing she was so upset you weren't here to take her call."

Chantelle had pointed out to me that this was receptionist lore—weather was always perfectly safe topic for soothing conversation. "Thank you, Melodie," I said.

When she looked a little embarrassed to be thanked, an awful suspicion leaped into my mind. "What else did you talk about?"

"Oh, this and that," said Melodie with an airy wave of a hand.

"Explicitly what this and that?"

"We may have discussed freeway shootings."

This was not good. No doubt the recent random gunfire on the freeways of Los Angeles had made the evening news in Wollegudgerie. Melodie would have been delighted to add her quota of gruesome details. I fixed her with a gimlet stare. "Anything else?"

Melodie pursed her lips, as if in deep thought. "I may have mentioned Dr. Braithwaite's accident on Sunset Boulevard."

"Bloody hell!"

"She was very interested," Melodie declared, obviously stung by my reaction. "You mom said she likes to know everything about your life here in L.A."

I shook my head, lost for words. I could see a harrowing telephone conversation coming up. Wouldn't it rot your socks?

EIGHT

As it was Tuesday afternoon in Los Angeles, it was Wednesday morning in Wollegudgerie. A plumbing disaster at the Wombat's Retreat had just occurred when I got Mum on the line. "Kylie, can't talk now. Water's absolutely pouring through the ceiling in the bottom hallway and Jack's no bloody good at all. He's running around like a chook with its head chopped off. I've got an emergency call in for Danny P., but you know how reliable he is."

Saved from a lecture! I'd been ready to deflect Mum by bringing up the subject of the Aussie TV show where my name had been mentioned. I was going to demand to know why nobody had told me about it. But now I blessed the pub's bodgy plumbing, which failed regularly, though not quite in so spectacular a way.

I immediately felt guilty. Disasters like this only seemed to occur when the place was chock-a-block with guests. And Danny Panopolous, Wollegudgerie's only plumber, was not fully dedicated to his trade. As Danny told anyone who'd listen, his real calling was in humorous writing.

At this point he'd always point at his truck, where the words THE PIPES OF PAN ARE CALLING appeared in large scarlet letters. "Get it?" Danny'd say. "The song, 'Danny Boy'? The pipes of Pan? Plumber Panopolous?" He'd shoot his heavy black eyebrows up and down. "Funny, eh?"

"Mum, I'll call you tomorrow," I said. "In the meantime, good luck with Danny P."

My mum snorted. "You know what I think—" she began, then

51

broke off. In the background I could hear Jack shouting something about the ceiling collapsing. "Holy mackerel!" said Mum. "I've got to go. Hooroo, love." The line went dead.

I felt a jab of regret I wasn't there to help out, and that Mum had to rely on Jack. But then, she had chosen him as future husband material, and they were officially engaged, though my Aunt Millie didn't think Mum would ever actually marry him.

I'd better get back to work. Moodily, I opened the Yarrow file Lonnie had given me. Then I was struck by the fact that here was another Jack. Mum's fiancé was Jack O'Connell: Oscar Braithwaite's nemesis was Jack Yarrow.

That got me musing about names. Jack had an abrupt, masculine sound. Kylie was softer, but it had a hard *k* to give it some weight. Ariana was perfect—elegant and contained.

Sometimes names didn't suit people. Sometimes they really did. Melodie certainly suited Melodie, and I couldn't imagine Lonnie called anything but Lonnie, but Fran was too mild for Fran. What would I rename Fran, if I had the power? Godzilla? Or some militant Teutonic name—say, Brunhilda. She didn't have the height for that moniker, but I could still visualize Fran as a pocket-size warrior queen, beaten-metal breastplate and all.

I grinned to myself as I elaborated on the picture in my mind, dressing my imaginary Fran for a leading role in a sword-and-sandal epic fantasy. On her red hair I placed a burnished copper helmet with horns. In one hand she held a round battle shield, in the other a sword with a gorgeously jeweled handle. Her face held a look of gloomy resolution, as she gazed, frowning, into a challenging future.

"What's so funny?" demanded the object of my flight of imagination. She had none of the accoutrements of a warrior queen, except maybe for the combative attitude and the frown.

"Not a thing, Fran. Just trying to be cheerful."

Fran gave a derisive grunt. Blimey, this sheila might be good-looking in a glum sort of way, but elegant she wasn't. She leaned over my desk to slap down a bunch of envelopes. "Mail."

"Thank you."

I sorted through them. Somehow, magically, the fact I'd moved to Los Angeles seemed to have got out into the world, and I was starting to get offers I supposedly couldn't refuse. It was amazing how many credit card companies found me worthy of special attention, and how many banks yearned to serve me in every possible financial way. Charities I'd never heard off begged for donations in heartbreaking terms.

"Ahem!" I became aware that Fran was still there, arms folded.

"Fran?"

"Storage of our disaster supplies," she said. "What have you done about it?"

"Fair go," I protested. "Why's it my job to find somewhere to store the stuff? You're the office manager, after all."

"There'd be somewhere, if you weren't here, Kylie." She pursed her lips, looking around my office reflectively. "For one thing, this room would be available. And then there's your bedroom—"

"Stop right there!"

Fran stopped, but her determined expression didn't change. We had a bit of a staring contest which Fran won because a vision of her as Brunhilda superimposed itself on the real person, and I had a bit of a giggle.

"I'm working hard to save all of our lives in the event of a terrorist attack or natural disaster," said Fran with affronted dignity. "Somehow you seem to find that amusing."

"Put it down to hysteria," I said. "These are trying times."

Fran tapped her foot. Clearly she was going nowhere until I came up with a storage plan of some sort. "Garden shed," I said. "You know, one of those green metal numbers. There's room in the backyard for it."

Fran's expression didn't lighten. "In the event of a gas attack, you'd go outside and die before you got to the gas masks. Same with germ warfare. You'd be fatally infected before you made it back into the building."

Crikey, she had a point there. "The shed wouldn't be for storage of your disaster supplies," I said quickly. "It'd be for the office supplies. Moving that stuff out to the shed would leave you an entire room to use."

Fran gave it a bit of deep thought. "Could work," she admitted at last. "When are we getting the shed?" Her frown, which had momentarily disappeared, returned. "I suppose you'll have to clear it with Ariana. That will take more time. Time we may not have. The essence of terrorism is the surprise attack. Could happen any moment."

I felt a jab of dinkum rage. First Fran wanted to get rid of me, just so she could free up some storage space. That was bad enough. Now she was implying I had to answer to Ariana for every little thing, even though I was the majority owner of Kendall & Creeling.

"I don't need to check with Ariana," I said coldly. "Go ahead and research what's available. I'll OK the order as soon as we decide the best shed to get."

"We decide?" said Fran, not willing to give a centimeter. "I am the office manager."

"Watch it," I warned.

There was a ten-second battle of wills, then Fran gave me a reluctant smile. "I'll get back to you," she said.

Fran left. I opened the Yarrow folder once more. I'd only glanced at it before, and hadn't realized what a fascinating record this bloke had. Apart from all his professional achievements and published works—there were pages of these—Lonnie had dug up some interesting criminal items. For example, there were a couple of charges of driving under the influence; two assaults, the victims in each case being women; plus one accusation of plagiarism, which actually made it to court but was settled just before the case started.

Professor Yarrow had been married three times. His first wife had died of a heart attack. Lonnie had noted there were no suspicious circumstances, as the woman had had a congenital heart problem. The second wife had been the victim in one of the assaults Yarrow had been arrested for, and she'd filed for divorce immediately after the attack. He was still married to his third wife, Winona Worsack, a noted medievalist. Lonnie had attached a brief outline of her career too. She seemed to be quite famous in her field. Next to her name Lonnie had written "old money" followed by three exclamation marks.

He'd also lifted photos from the Internet. Here was Professor Yarrow at this conference or that; here was Yarrow appearing on *60 Minutes*; here the professor and his wife were meeting with the President...

I studied his face. Jack Yarrow had a high, domed forehead. He brushed his thinning hair forward in a sort of Roman Caesar style. He had a small, puggish nose; a tight, thin-lipped mouth; and slightly pro-tuberant pale eyes. There were two or three shots of him with Winona Worsack. She favored flowing clothes and an ethereal expression. Her straight, dark hair reached her shoulders, and she had those extremely long, thin hands that I always imagined would be cold, like the touch of a skeleton.

I sighed. Time for some serious study. Rube Wasinsky had given me some general sources for information on marsupials, and Lonnie had searched the Internet for more material, so I had a lot of reading to do before I turned up at the biology department at UCLA tomorrow as Kylie Kendall, graduate student, just off a plane from Australia and thrilled to be there in time to rub shoulders with the luminaries at next week's Global Marsupial Symposium.

I started with quokkas since Oscar had such an interest in them. I read:

> Quokkas are the size of a domestic cat, and have rounded bodies, a short tail and a face much more flattened than other wallabies. One of the first Australian mammals seen by Europeans, were first sighted in 1658 when Dutch mariner Samuel Volckertzoon wrote of discovering something like a wild cat on Rottnest Island.

I stopped to consider Volckertzoon as a name. It made Kendall look awfully boring. I wondered if his friends called him Volcky... I gave myself a mental slap. Back to work.

ⵒ

By the time Chantelle came to pick me up, I was rather better informed about marsupials in general and quokkas in particular, than

I had ever intended to be.

I gave her a hug and climbed into her red Jeep. She loved bright colors, and was wearing a lemony outfit tonight, which set off her satiny coffee skin.

"You look bonzer," I said.

She leaned over to give me a kiss. "Not so bad yourself."

"Did you know," I remarked as we set off, "that quokkas breed once a year and produce a single joey?"

"Fascinating," said Chantelle, with heavy irony, "but why are you telling me this?"

"It was hard yakka learning all this info for my new case," I said, "so the least I can do is toss a few facts into a conversation, don't you think?"

She gave me a sideways glance. "I'd rather you didn't."

"Fair enough." Then a thought struck me. "You didn't ask me what a quokka is."

"I didn't need to."

"Melodie?

Chantelle grinned. "Need you ask?"

I shook my head. The receptionists' network was frighteningly efficient. One could only hope it never occurred to terrorists to infiltrate it.

Chantelle was an excellent driver, so I could relax and enjoy the scenery, which was mostly made up of other vehicles hurrying to apparently superurgent destinations.

"Tell me all about Dr. Penny," said Chantelle.

"Didn't Melodie cover everything? She and Pen Braithwaite had quite a conversation."

"Melodie wasn't up close and personal with her like you, honey." She reached over to squeeze my knee. "Did she try to jump your bones? The word is, she's insatiable."

"She didn't put the hard word on me, if that's what you mean."

"She will," said Chantelle with perfect conviction.

"Crikey, do you really think so?"

"Count on it."

Yerks!

⊃

The premiere was being held at a cinema in Westwood Village, near the UCLA campus. Chantelle knew every trick about parking, and found a spot on a nearby suburban street. We set off walking. The closer we got to the cinema, the more crowded the footpaths became, until we turned a corner and there it was, all decked out like a Chrissie tree.

This place put the Regal Picture Palace in Wollegudgerie to shame. Lights scintillated, music played, fans kept up a roar, presumably of approval, as limousines pulled up to disgorge VIPs. There was a constant flicker of camera flashes as photographs were taken of anything that moved. There was even a red carpet for the stars to tread on as they made their way inside.

Scads of people were pressing up against the barriers erected to keep them from getting too close to the arriving celebrities. TV stations had vans parked nearby, and I recognized an on-air reporter I'd often watched on the local news. He was much shorter than I'd thought and was frowning ferociously, not at all like the cheery personality he projected on the screen.

Chantelle halted beside the barrier preventing fans from spilling onto the beginning of the red carpet. "Why all the security?" I asked.

"Celebrity dread," she said, fossicking through her purse. "Drat! I've got to have the passes somewhere, or we won't get in."

"What are the celebrities dreading?"

"Ah-hah!" said Chantelle, flourishing two squares of cardboard.

"Are those tickets for tonight?" inquired a hopeful voice. "I'll give you a hundred dollars for them."

The voice belonged to a weedy little guy who was oddly dressed in an extraordinarily grubby once-white outfit consisting of many floating panels. I reckoned his face was made up to look like a corpse that had been rotting for some time. Seeing me staring at him, he said, "I'm a *Bloodblot* ghoul. Didn't you see the first movie?"

"Sorry, missed it."

The ghoul's attention was back on Chantelle's passes. "A hundred and fifty," he said. "Each. That's my best offer."

"Two hundred," someone called, pushing through the crowd in our direction. There was a general murmur of interest.

"Let's get out of here," said Chantelle, seizing my elbow and heading for two overmuscled security guards. She waved the passes under their noses. "We're with United Flair."

They did the squinty-eye bit, and then allowed us to join the privileged people on the red carpet. "There's Sigfried Smithey," Chantelle hissed at me. "Not A-list yet, but they're saying this movie should give him a good push in that direction." She scanned the slowly-moving queue of people. "Look over there, beside Demi Moore—that's the newest teen sensation, Godfrey Free."

"That's Demi Moore?" I said. "Crikey, she looks as fit as a flea."

"Fitter," said Chantelle. "If she's going to run with a young crowd, she has to be."

"What's this celebrity dread thing you were talking about before?" I asked.

"They dread everything," said Chantelle with a touch of scorn. "Celebrities dread being the target of kidnappers—preferably with some link to foreign terrorists—who'll demand millions of dollars to set them free. Then they dread that they're not famous enough to be kidnapped in the first place. And of course they dread not having hordes of paparazzi after them."

"Stars are always complaining about paparazzi," I pointed out.

"They don't mean it," said Chantelle. "United Flair has one client who insists we alert the paparazzi every time he goes out in public. Last week he had a knock-down, drag-out fight with one. Broke the guy's nose and his camera." She shook her head admiringly. "You can't buy that kind of publicity."

"Chantelle! Long time no see!" was shrieked in our direction. The young woman's long hair was a rich red, her hot pink dress was miniscule, her physique anorexic, her delight at seeing Chantelle almost alarming.

"Ashlee, hi," said Chantelle without a great deal of enthusiasm.

If this was the Ashlee I thought it was, then the teeth she was flashing were of the snap-on variety.

Ashlee had turned her fevered attention on me. "And I suppose this is your special friend, Chantelle?"

"G'day. Kylie Kendall's the name."

The snap-ons disappeared. "Oh," Ashlee said, "you're foreign."

"Actually, I'm an American citizen," I said, "thanks to the fact my dad was a Yank, and I was born here in L.A."

"But your funny accent—Cockney, isn't it?" Ashlee looked quite pleased with her powers of perception. "Cockney," she repeated with emphasis.

"My funny accent's Australian," I said. "Australian."

"Oh?" Ashlee didn't seemed convinced. "It sounds like Cockney to me."

"It isn't," snapped Chantelle. "We've got to move along. See you later, OK?" She watched Ashlee totter off on her very high heels. "Occasionally, you get a bad apple in the receptionist pool," she said gloomily.

"Ashlee's a bad apple?"

Chantelle grinned at me. "Rotten to the core."

NINE

Very early next morning I kissed Chantelle goodbye and set out to walk the couple of kilometers to Kendall & Creeling. I'd got into the habit of leaving a set of casual clothes at her place, so if I stayed the night, I could change into shorts, T-shirt and running shoes, bundle whatever I'd been wearing into a shoulder bag and jog—or more likely, briskly walk—back home.

Because I wanted to go through my notes before going to UCLA, I hadn't intended to spend the night at Chantelle's apartment. However, as *Bloodblot Horror II* had scared the living daylights out of me, the thought of being alone in the dark after what I'd seen on the screen had given me the heebie-jeebies. If I'd had an inkling of how bad it was going to be, I'd have skipped the screening, the way the stars of the movie had.

Last night, after a reception thingo in the lobby of the cinema, people had started to move into the theater. At that point I'd noticed the celebrities drifting in the opposite direction.

"Where are they going?" I'd asked. "Is there special seating for them?"

"They're leaving," said Chantelle. "The stars of *Bloodblot II* came to be seen by the fans, not to view the movie. They'll slip out the back way, hop into their limos, and beat it."

After enduring the vile, gruesome images of *Bloodblot Horror II*, I'd wished I'd done the same. Chantelle, of course, had taken the carnage in her stride. I'd clutched her hand and shut my eyes at the worst spots, but even the screams from the audience didn't drown out the ghastly sound effects of slicing, dicing, and disemboweling. One good thing, though—I'd had no opportunity to brood about Ariana and the Natalie sheila.

Later, Chantelle had been warmly appreciative of the effect *Bloodblot* had had on me. "You're clingy tonight, honey. I like that."

"I wouldn't call it clingy," I protested. "It's just that I'm a bit of a scaredy-cat when it comes to horror movies."

Chantelle's eyes had lit up. "There's some great ones I'd love you to see. For instance, the DVD of *Death Gurgle* is out next week. And another really good one, *Eviscerate,* is already in the stores, and—"

"Are you serious? Or are you teasing me?"

Chantelle had given me a ravishing smile. "Both," she'd said.

Now, in the early-morning light, the butchery of *Bloodblot Horror II* didn't have the same clout. I felt a little embarrassed that I'd allowed a mere movie to frighten me. Hell's bells, there were enough real horrors in the world without worrying about fictional ones.

I turned my thoughts to the major challenge ahead of me. Today I was lobbing into UCLA in my undercover role. Before I left for the campus, I'd just have time to shower, dress, gulp down a bowl of porridge, and do a lightning check of the information any real graduate student would know. I reminded myself I'd have to devote a few minutes to soothing Julia Roberts. It seemed to annoy her intensely when I stayed out all night. It wasn't lack of food, as I always left her ample provisions, so I'd decided it was that she missed me. This gave me a warm feeling.

"Did you miss me, Jules?" I said as soon as I opened Kendall & Creeling's front door.

Julia Roberts, who was reclining on Melodie's reception desk gymnastically washing her nethers, paused with one hind leg high in the air. She considered my question for all of three seconds, then resumed washing.

"Hiding your true emotions, I see. Well done, Jules. It's the way to go these days."

"Good morning, Kylie."

My heart did a rollover. "Crikey! You gave me a fright."

Ariana smiled faintly. "Sorry. I came in early to catch up on some work."

"Are you OK?" This was the question I'd told myself not to ask, but this morning, looking at her white, drawn face, I couldn't stop myself.

I thought Ariana would brush me off, but she didn't. "Yesterday I was—I was taken aback. Penelope Braithwaite stirred up old memories. My apologies for leaving everything in the meeting to you. It wasn't very professional of me."

The impulse to comfort her was almost overwhelming. But if I took two steps and put my arms around her, I was pretty sure she'd freeze me out so fast my head would spin. Instead, I offered the great Aussie restorative, used in situations ranging from a simple case of fatigue right through to the total loss of one's home in a bushfire. "How about a cuppa?"

"Tea? I'd rather have coffee."

I followed Ariana to the kitchen, Julia Roberts bringing up the rear. Once there, Jules parked herself in front of her empty food dish and looked meaningfully at me.

"You ate all the chicken and liver?" I said. Julia Roberts twitched her whiskers impatiently. Last night's dinner was old news. Today was a new gastronomical adventure.

While getting tuna-and-whitefish bites for her breakfast snack, I noticed Fran had posted a diagram on the cupboard door detailing escape routes from the building. TAKE TIME TO CHECK THE LOCATION OF YOUR NEAREST EXIT she had put in large scarlet letters along the bottom. Since, as I'd pointed out to Fran earlier, the choice was the front door or the back door, this information did seem rather unnecessary. I said so to Ariana.

"Visitors to the building may not know the location of the exits," she said with her usual cool logic.

I had to concede she was right. An outraged meow brought my attention back to the most important item on the agenda, breakfast for Jules. She watched intently as I poured a moderate measure of tuna-and-whitefish bites into her bowl. I swear she was counting the little fish-shaped things. Apparently the total wasn't to her liking, because she narrowed her eyes.

"A larger helping, Jules? Of course. What could I have been thinking of?"

Ariana gave a small laugh. "You need to acquire a dog, Kylie. Gussie treats me with great respect, firmly convinced I'm the head of the household."

Ariana's German shepherd was the perfect combination of strength, intelligence, and grace. Gussie was fiercely protective of Ariana, but to those she knew and trusted, there couldn't be a sweeter, more even-tempered dog. And Gussie had a bonzer sense of humor. I'd seen her grin when she found something amusing.

"What's that saying about dogs and cats?" I remarked, filling my kettle at the tap. "To dogs, humans are absolute monarchs, but to cats, they're servants?"

"Something like that." Ariana looked at me over the rim of her coffee mug. Her face was so pale that her eyes, if it were possible, seemed even bluer than usual. "You must be curious."

She didn't need to elaborate. "I confess I am," I said.

Ariana grimaced. "I don't blame you. I overreacted and made it seem more significant than it really was."

I didn't say anything.

Ariana said, "Would you do something for me?"

I looked at her warily. "Possibly. What?"

"Don't pursue it, Kylie, please. It's better for both of us if you forget the whole thing."

I gazed at her for a long moment. "I didn't Google her name. I didn't do anything to find out who she was."

"Thank you for that."

"But I'd be lying if I said I'd forget. Obviously whoever Natalie is, she's important to you. That makes her important to me."

I was jolted to see tears in Ariana's eyes. She blinked rapidly, then took a breath. Whatever she might have been about to say was lost when Melodie bounced into the kitchen, having arrived at work astonishingly early by her standards.

"Quip's written a play!" she announced. "It's going to be staged in a little theater on La Cienega Boulevard. That's just the beginning. Quip's thinking off-Broadway." She paused, smiling, to let us absorb this, then added, "Fran's coming in before work with audition scripts so I can go over them before tonight!"

Melodie fanned her blond hair fetchingly in a head toss she'd got down to a fine art. "The stage is real acting," she declared. "You and the audience magically bond in a profound dramatic relationship. Live theater challenges an actor to dig deep, to reveal the hidden depths of her craft."

"Good morning, Melodie," I said.

"Oh, hi, Kylie. Hi, Ariana. Isn't it great news?"

"Very exciting," said Ariana, picking up her mug from the counter. She turned at the doorway to say, "Kylie, when you get back from your first day at UCLA I'd like to hear how it went."

"Right-oh," I said, offhand.

I wanted to follow her to her office. I wanted to say, "Tell me, Ariana. Tell me what it is that makes you cry." I wanted to, but I wouldn't because pushing her that way could destroy the tentative relationship that was growing up between us.

"You're going undercover today?" Melodie clasped her hands as if in prayer. "College types are real smart, Kylie."

"You mean they'll see through me?"

Melodie considered this for a moment. "You're not born to act, like me. Larry, my agent, says it's in the blood."

"Acting is genetic?"

"Well, there's natural talent, of course. Fortunately I have that in spades. But it's not enough. Talent has to be honed, techniques perfected. Dance classes, speech classes, movement classes…" She shook her head. "'Fraid you're behind the eight ball, Kylie, before you even start."

"Hardly seems worthwhile to even try," I said, shaking my head in turn.

Melodie patted my arm consolingly. "It's real lucky you're an Aussie," she said. "Like, you're foreign, and you talk funny."

"That's exactly what Snap-on Ashlee said to me last night."

"Ashlee was at the *Bloodblot* premiere?" Melodie seemed seriously irked.

"She was. Accosted Chantelle and me on the red carpet."

A scowl darkened Melodie's face. "Ashlee swore to me she couldn't get passes. She lied. And she knew how much I wanted to go."

Wondering how Ashlee would have access to these prized tickets to premieres, I asked where she worked.

"She's a receptionist at Crucial Casting, Incorporated," said Melodie moodily. "Ashlee knows I'm a major fan of Sigfried Smithey's. She could have helped a sister receptionist out—but no!" Melodie sagged against the kitchen counter. "Why? I ask myself, why?"

"Bad apple," I said, adding with a grin, "Probably rotten to the core."

"Damn," Melodie said, suddenly invigorated. "I'd do anything to stop her hearing about the auditions for Quip's play." She stamped her foot in vexation. "It's too late to put a gag order out."

"The receptionist network can censor information?"

Melodie tsk-tsked. "It's not censorship. That would be un-American. It's more a selective hush-up."

"What does it matter if Ashlee hears about the auditions anyway?" I inquired.

"She thinks she can act," said Melodie with deep derision. "Act! Even you'd be better than Ashlee."

"Thank you, Melodie."

Melodie ignored my sarcastic tone. "It may not be too late after all," she said thoughtfully. "A careless-with-the-truth strategy might still work."

"Receptionists lie?"

"Oh, please," said Melodie. "It's a basic requirement. You don't think it's always a good morning or a good afternoon, do you? And when we say someone's in a meeting, do you really believe that's always true?"

While I was digesting this, Melodie caught sight of Jules, who was washing her whiskers. Fastidious things, cats. Melodie put both her hands to her head in a dramatic gesture. "I feel a psychic moment coming on."

Jules halted the whisker cleaning to look at her with a quizzical expression. "Julia Roberts!" Melodie exclaimed. "I sense Lonnie's door is open. Why don't you mosey down the hall and make yourself comfortable in his chair? He'll really appreciate it."

"You opened Lonnie's door?"

Melodie smiled meltingly. "Could you doubt it?"

"You're dinky-di evil," I said.

ᔑ

I'd sussed out exactly where the biology department was on my first visit to UCLA, so I didn't have to wander around looking lost but could make a beeline straight to the building. The interior was what I mentally labeled "institution decor." The long corridors were lined with anonymous doors, each with a glass panel of frosted glass. The flooring was that grayish composite stuff everyone knows has been selected because it doesn't show the dirt that much and is easy to clean.

Every now and then there was a notice board on the wall. I stopped at one to read instructions for actions to take in the event of a major earthquake. Thoroughly unsettled by this information, I made for Dr. Rubin Wasinsky's office.

I don't mind admitting my nerves were snapping like old rubber bands, but Rube smoothed the way. He introduced me to the people in the biology department as someone fresh off the plane from Western Australia and quite jet-lagged. This gave me a reasonable excuse if I made some awful slipup, such as making a total hash of a biological term, or giving some marsupial the wrong Latin name.

Actually, I was aiming to steer clear of scientific names as much as possible, as my Latin was pretty well limited to *nil desperandum, tempus fugit, caveat emptor,* and *carpe diem.* Although I could imagine there might be opportunities to casually comment on not despairing, the tendency of time to fly, the warning for buyers to beware, and the philosophy of seizing the day, I sensed that occasion was not now.

Yesterday, Rube had given me a rundown on who was who in the department, so my main role today was to try to fit names to faces. One person with whom Rube said it was vital I cultivate a working relationship was administrative assistant, Georgia Tapp. She was a plump, motherly woman with faded brown hair, a cloyingly sweet expression, and dimples to rival Lonnie's. Then I met Zoran Pestle, thin and intense, a colleague of Rube's who was on the committee running the symposium.

"And this is Erin Fogarty," said Rube. "Erin, meet Kylie Kendall, visiting doctoral student from Australia."

"G'day," I said, regarding her with interest. This was the graduate assistant who had upped and shot through on Oscar Braithwaite, only to turn up later here at UCLA, working with Jack Yarrow.

Erin Fogarty was a gangling young woman with a weak chin and high color. Her best feature seemed to be her short, curly hair, which shone with copper highlights.

"Hi," she said, eyeing me narrowly. "Will you be working with Professor Yarrow?"

"Kylie is here for ten weeks to work on a research paper with me," said Rube.

"Great," Erin said, visibly perking up. It was clear she wanted no competition as far as Professor Yarrow was concerned.

I'd assumed Erin would be an Aussie, since she'd been working out in the field with Oscar in Western Australia, but obviously I was wrong, as this sheila had a twangy American accent.

Rube resumed the introductions to the members of the faculty, with me trotting along compliantly the way I thought a jet-lagged overseas student would. Professor Yarrow himself I glimpsed from afar, rushing along as though on very important business.

"Always in a hurry, like the White Rabbit in Alice," Rube remarked disparagingly.

"Probably not as lovable," I said.

"Whoa. Bonus person," said Rube, catching sight of someone down the hall. I was beginning to really appreciate his wit. "You're in luck, Kylie. Here comes Winona Worsack, Yarrow's wife, paying an unannounced connubial visit."

"Unannounced? She doesn't trust the bloke?"

Rube's smile had a touch of malice. "Not as far as she can throw him. She routinely nurses dark suspicions about any young woman with proximity to her husband."

As befitting a medievalist, Winona Worsack wore a floor length, flowing dress and had her dark hair loose on her shoulders. She sort of glided along, hands clasped at waist level, as though on hidden wheels. When she got close to us, she switched on a brief smile. "Rubin."

"Winona."

She gave me an appraising once-over and put the brakes on. "Hello," she said, "I don't believe we've met."

"G'day. Kylie Kendall's the name."

"Just visiting?"

"For ten weeks," I said, "working with Dr. Wasinsky."

"With Rubin? Excellent."

"But I hope to learn so much from Professor Yarrow too," I said with warmth. "He's such a wonderful man."

Winona Worsack raised her eyebrows. "Indeed?"

It's possible some of Melodie's evil had rubbed off on me, because I found myself continuing in the same breathless tone, "It's a dinkum honor to meet such a world-renowned authority on marsupials. I can hardly believe it's happening to me, a little sheila from Oz."

"Kylie's seriously jet-lagged," said Rube, giving me a warning glance. "Arrived from Australia this morning."

Yarrow's wife looked as if something decidedly rotten had been thrust under her nostrils. She got herself in gear and started to move off. "Delightful to meet you, Kylie," she murmured, not meaning a single word of it.

"It was bonzer meeting you too," I called after her.

Rube gave me a severe look, then broke into a wide grin. "Bad Kylie," he said.

TEN

Today Rube had abandoned his brown cardigan, and was wearing wrinkled brown trousers and an old tweed jacket with leather patches on the elbows. I was in student garb, jeans and T-shirt. Things were going swimmingly for me at the Department of Organismic Biology, Ecology and Evolution. Of course I'd hooted when Rube told me that was the full title of the biology department, but he'd assured me it was true.

So far this morning I'd met a whole lot of people, and hadn't put my foot in my mouth once. This was probably because I limited myself to "G'day" and a shy, modest smile. At least, I started off with my version of a shy, modest smile, but between introductions Rube Wasinsky chortled and said it made me look startlingly simple-minded. I then switched to an expression of thoughtful gravity.

Rube and I were heading back to Professor Yarrow's office to see if he was in residence so I could finally meet him, when the sounds of a loud altercation rang down the corridor.

"It's a crime against nature!" exclaimed a shrill voice. "Unnatural!"

"Codswallop! You're an abysmally stupid woman."

"Uh-oh," said Rube. "Pen's on the warpath."

"Homosexuality is a perversion! A gay animal is a sinful animal!"

We rounded the corner to find Pen and Georgia Tapp toe-to-toe, but not nose-to-nose, as Pen Braithwaite loomed over the administrative assistant. Height was not the only contrast between them. Georgia wore a neat pink dress, stockings, and moderate high heels. Pen had on ancient jeans and man's shirt with the sleeves rolled up to the elbows.

A small crowd had collected, and some were calling out comments and helpful advice.

Hands on hips, her well-upholstered form rigid with outrage, Georgia threw back her head, flared her nostrils, and declared, "Any homosexual animal should be put to death before it can pervert others of its breed."

Pen snorted, her nostrils similarly flared. Her tawny hair seemed almost to put out sparks. "Put plainly, you're an idiot. Do you think a lesbian sheep says to herself, 'I'm a bad, wicked sheep. I'll turn to the dark side and seduce that innocent ewe over there.'"

"How disgusting," spluttered Georgia.

Pen thrust her chin out with even more belligerence. "Open your closed, ossified mind, Georgia, and read the research. Homosexuality, bisexuality—it's a normal part of nature."

Shaking her head violently, Georgia declared, "I'll never believe that. Never!"

"Believe it. It's been documented—well-documented. There are homosexual ostriches. There are homosexual walruses. There are homosexual sage grouse. There are homosexual—"

"Arrgh!" Georgia clapped her hands over her ears. "Stop this filthy talk."

"What's going on here?" demanded an imperious voice. It was Jack Yarrow himself, his expression a blend of ire and indignation. He gaze swept the assembled spectators. "Show's over, ladies and gentlemen," he said with a sardonic sneer. "Back to work." No one moved.

I compared the man with the photographs I'd seen in the file Lonnie had given me. They'd clearly shown Yarrow's domed forehead with its Roman Empire hairstyle vainly attempting to hide his growing baldness. His small, flattish nose was the same, as were his prominent washed-out blue-gray eyes and thin-lipped mouth. What hadn't been indicated was his excellent physique. He had a well-muscled, flat-stomached body with wide shoulders and narrow waist. And in person his skin was peculiar, being thick and white and somehow creepy, as though if I put a finger out and pushed his cheek, my finger would leave a distinct crater. Errk!

"Oh, Professor Yarrow," twittered Georgia, "Dr. Braithwaite viciously attacked me because of my deeply held beliefs."

Yarrow flicked a contemptuous look at Pen, who, arms folded, was leaning serenely against the wall. "I'm sure you held your ground against Dr. Braithwaite, Georgia. Her arguments are often fallacious."

"Is that so?" said Pen, straightening up.

"Have you got a moment, Jack?" Rube interposed hastily. "I'd like you to meet Kylie Kendall, my new graduate student, who'll be pitching in to help us with the Global Marsupial Symposium."

Yarrow glanced at me, then took another look. A smile appeared on his mouth—his eyes remained cold. "My wife mentioned meeting you. Do come into my office and we can have a chat about your time with us."

When Rube went to come too, Yarrow said, "I'll send her back to you later."

Rube looked worried, which mirrored how I felt. This was the crucial test, where I fooled Yarrow into believing I was who I said I was. Stone the crows, I wished I'd studied the biology stuff more closely. This bloke could trip me up without really trying. And my mind had gone blank. Blimey! What was the exact name of the research paper I was supposed to be involved in? I'd have to find some way to deflect him from asking too many pointed questions.

I meekly followed Professor Yarrow into his room, which was very well-appointed, with a thick maroon carpet, a heavy desk which was obviously not standard issue, and walls lined with custom-made bookshelves.

He closed the door behind us, then sat down behind his desk and waved me to a chair. "Welcome to UCLA, Kylie."

"G'day, Professor Yarrow."

A small, frosty smile on his lips, he gave me a slow once-over. He nodded. "Well, well, some good does come out of the antipodes."

"Is that a compliment?"

He looked surprised. "You may read it as such. Why?"

"Just wondered if I would thank you, or take offense and counterattack."

"I believe I'd prefer a thank-you," he said drily. "University of Western Australia, is it?"

"That's right."

"Then you'd know Howard Leadbeater."

Trick question. Good thing I'd thought to ask Lonnie to research the faculty for past and present VIPs in the world of biological science. "I know of him. He's a world authority on marsupials, but of course I never had the chance to meet him. He'd fallen off the perch long before I got there."

"Fallen off the perch?" His mouth twisted in a most unpleasant way. "How quaint."

"Thank you, Professor Yarrow."

The deep sincerity in my voice brought a slight frown to his pale forehead. "Australians as a race are admirable," he intoned, "except for your propensity to use diminutives and excessively colorful colloquialisms."

"Hang on a mo," I said. "Fair crack of the whip. Aussies save a lot of time with those shortened words. Like, would you mind if I called you Prof?"

"I believe I would."

"Right-oh," I said. "Professor it is."

"Now, the research paper you're working on with Dr. Wasinsky…?"

I put my hand to my mouth to cover a fake yawn. "Sorry, Professor Yarrow, just got to L.A., so I'm a bit jet-lagged."

"The title of your paper?"

Crikey, this bloke was persistent. "Distribution and Movement Patterns of Urban Platypuses," I said, then had a stab at the appropriate Latin label. "*Ornithorhynchus anatinus* in the creeks and rivers near urban areas."

The platypus was, as Rube had pointed out to me, a notoriously shy animal, so the discovery of platypuses living in waterways close to large towns and cities was an eye-opener.

"Monotremes, the lowest order of mammals," the professor said with little enthusiasm. Rube had deliberately chosen a field he knew Yarrow wasn't particularly interested in, so that he wouldn't be likely to ask probing questions or follow-up on the work I was supposed to be doing.

"But so fascinating!" I exclaimed. "I'm captivated by the fact that the platypus has its own specially adapted species of tick."

Professor Yarrow got up and came around my side of the desk. Putting a hand on my shoulder, he said, "Ah, the enthusiasm of youth." His grip tightened. "Such zest for life is so attractive in a young woman."

While I was considering my options—play along or unceremoniously brush his fingers off—the office door abruptly opened.

"Jack," said Winona Worsack, gliding into the room, "am I interrupting something?"

Yarrow ripped his hand off me fast. "My dear, of course not."

His wife looked pointedly at my shoulder, then at him. "I thought we might lunch together, darling," she said. "Unless you have something more pressing to do…"

"An excellent idea. Excellent." He turned to me, all business. "As I was saying, I'm sure your time with us will be most valuably spent with Dr. Wasinsky. Unfortunately, my attention will be largely taken up by the symposium, so if you have any concerns or worries I'm afraid you'll have to channel them through my assistant, Ms. Tapp."

From her expression, Winona wasn't having any wool pulled over her eyes. "You always manage to make yourself available when you feel it necessary, Jack." She darted a glance at me. "I'm sure if—"

"Kylie," I said obligingly.

"I'm sure if Kylie needs your attention, she'll get it."

"The Global Marsupial Symposium is all-consuming at the moment, Winona," he said with a frown. "I scarcely have time for my own work, let alone worrying about supervision of a visiting graduate student."

I took this as my cue to hop it. "Bye, Prof. And nice to see you again, Mrs. Yarrow."

He looked pained. She looked irritated.

He said, "Professor, if you don't mind."

She said, "I don't use Yarrow. You may refer to me as Dr. Worsack."

"Sorry."

I left her glaring at him—I was betting lunch wasn't going to be much fun—and set off for Rube Wasinsky's office. I was getting a feel for the geography of the place, so I found it without too much trouble.

Rube's furnishings were nothing like Yarrow's: standard-issue desk, rickety bookcase, a floor of the same material as the hallway. Pen Braithwaite was sitting in his chair with her feet up on the desk. She was wearing quite the ugliest sandals I had ever seen, consisting of many khaki-colored straps attached to a massive sole.

"Rube's off getting me coffee," she said. "How'd it go with Yarrow?"

I recounted the events, including his wife's entrance. Pen snickered happily. "Narrow escape there, Kylie. In two shakes his hand would have been wandering south."

"Good thing Dr. Worsack came in, then."

"Winona? What do you think of her?"

"I haven't had much time to form an opinion, but I reckon she doesn't like me."

"Winona's a professional medievalist," said Pen contemptuously. "Always in costume with those long dresses. Even plays the bloody lyre, would you believe? Jack Yarrow married her for her money, but God knows why she married him. Though I hear he's a randy bastard…"

"He has quite a good body," I observed.

Pen swung her feet off the table and sat up. "You're bi?"

"Not a chance."

Pen sank back in the chair and put her feet up again. "Your partner, Ariana, is a very attractive woman."

I agreed this was so in my best noncommittal tone.

"Has she thawed out yet?" Pen inquired.

It seemed best to play dumb. "I'm sorry?"

"Ariana gave me the big freeze after I mentioned Natalie Ives."

"She was a bit withdrawn," I conceded.

Pen let out a bellow of laughter. "Withdrawn! She near froze my titties off!"

I winced. Pen's voice would carry quite a way. "I'm sure she didn't mean it personally," I said.

"I didn't know the Ives woman," said Pen. "She was before my time.

I joined the UCLA faculty just as she was retiring."

My pulse rate went up. Maybe I'd find out who Natalie was without really trying. "Oh?" I said. "So she was in the psychology department with you?"

"Psychology? What made you think that? She was an English scholar. Very noted in her field of—what was it?" Pen gazed at the ceiling for inspiration, which came almost immediately. "Nineteenth-century British literature," she announced triumphantly.

Rube swept in with three coffees on a cardboard tray. "Thought you'd be here," he said, handing me one of the thick paper cups, "but you should be making good use of your time chatting up Georgia Tapp."

I expected a flare-up from Pen at the mention of the Tapp woman's name, but she was smiling. "That was fun this morning," she said. "I love getting up Georgia's nose. She's so predictable."

"I think you should handle her with kid gloves," said Rube. "Georgia's the rigid type who'll snap one day, bring a gun to work and start blasting away." He added severely, "And you, Pen, will be her number one target."

Pen's grin widened. "Kylie, you should have been here the day I pointed out to Georgia the dangers of repressing her sexuality, and made some concrete suggestions about how she might loosen up. She damn near imploded!"

"I thought I'd start with Erin Fogarty," I said. "Oscar said he thought she'd passed on his quokka research to Jack Yarrow."

Pen's smile disappeared. "She's having an affair with Yarrow, the silly little fool. Working her butt off researching papers she fondly believes will be published with her name under his. That won't happen. Professor Jack Yarrow is the only author that will appear. There'll be no mention of her substantial contributions."

"What if she makes a fuss?" I asked.

Rube grunted. "Erin Fogarty's a student: Yarrow's a renowned professor. Say she goes public and accuses him of taking all the credit when she did most of the work. Who'd listen to her?" His mouth turned down. "Unfortunately, it's not all that rare in the academic world, but

Yarrow's a particularly egregious offender."

"He's a bastard," said Pen. "You're right, Kylie. Concentrate on the Fogarty girl." She mused for a moment. "You could seduce her. Pillow talk's useful."

"Crikey, you're asking a lot!"

Pen raised her eyebrows. "You're not open to a little hanky-panky?"

"You've got that right."

"Tsk," said Pen. "Subjugating your natural, healthy sexual instincts is unwise."

"I'll risk it."

Pen gave me a slow smile. "A risk taker," she said. "I like that."

ELEVEN

I ran my quarry to ground in a little office about the size of a broom cupboard. Her lanky body was perched on the edge of a chair as she gazed fixedly into the screen of a laptop. When she looked up, I said with a friendly smile, "G'day. I'm Kylie Kendall. We met earlier."

"Oh, hi."

"You're so lucky," I said, "to be working with Professor Yarrow." I pouted a bit. "I'm stuck with Dr. Wasinsky. I mean, don't get me wrong. He's nice enough, but he's not a world-famous authority like Professor Yarrow."

Erin Fogarty's cheeks flushed, apparently with pleasure at this praise of her idol. "Professor Yarrow is a wonderful man. My dreams came true when I got the opportunity to come to UCLA to be part of his groundbreaking research into *Setonix brachyurus.*"

Personally, I'd have called a quokka a quokka, but if it made Erin happy to use Latin, it was all right by me. "There's got to be a meganumber of graduate students dying to work with someone as prestigious as the professor, but he chose you."

Her blush spread to include her weak chin and long neck. "In fact, you're right. He'd in such demand." She clasped her hands. "But I was the lucky one."

Uninvited, I plunked myself down in the only other chair in the cramped space. Aiming for a tone somewhere between admiration and envy, I leaned forward to say, "I'm guessing luck had nothing to do with it, Erin. I reckon you stood out from the pack, and that's why he picked you."

Her glossy chestnut curls seem to shimmer with added light. "It's nice of you to say so. Actually, Professor Yarrow—he's asked me to call him Jack in private—did say he especially valued the depth of my knowledge in the area."

Stone the crows! This poor sheila was head over heels, no worries. "So you studied quokkas in the wild?" I asked.

She bobbed her head. "Extensively. I spent months in Western Australia observing both the island and mainland colonies."

"You can't beat research in the field," I said. "Who were you working with?"

Her face clouded. "Dr. Oscar Braithwaite. Have you heard of him?"

"You mean the bloke who's going to speak next week at the symposium on the quokka question?"

"Yes." Her lips tightened. "He's already in L.A. In fact, he came to see me this morning. It was very embarrassing."

"Really?" I said in a neutral tone. "Why embarrassing?"

I made a mental note to find out why Oscar hadn't mentioned he intended to front up to Erin Fogarty. Maybe he'd decided to drop in on the spur of the moment. I recalled wondering, during my very first meeting with Oscar, if he'd had a personal interest in his graduate assistant.

Erin was hesitating, obviously torn between sharing the goss with me and keeping it to herself. Goss won. "Actually," she said, "when I was in Australia, Dr. Braithwaite paid me special attention…"

"He was keen on you?"

Her blush, which had faded, rushed back. Scarlet-faced, she said, "Nothing happened, of course, but I knew how he felt."

"You didn't return his affections?"

She drew back, affronted. "Oh! How could I?"

"Professional scruples held you back?" I ventured.

Erin shook her head. "You haven't seen him, have you? Oscar Braithwaite's hairy, very hairy. In fact, he's the hairiest man I've ever met."

"It'd be like dating a gorilla?"

This elicited a small smile. "Something like that."

"Bad sitch," I said. "What did you do?"

"Well, actually…" She paused, her lips compressed. Then, deciding to fill me in, she went on, "It was at this point Professor Yarrow contacted me."

"Crikey! He contacted you? You mean you didn't have to apply to come to UCLA?"

My admiring wonder had the desired effect. She turned a pleased pink. "Isn't it amazing? Professor Yarrow said he'd asked around in academic circles, and I'd been highly recommended to him."

"So you gave Dr. Braithwaite the heave-ho and came over here?"

Erin seemed a bit taken aback at this blunt assessment. "Actually," she said—she seemed to like that word—"there was another reason I couldn't work with Oscar any longer." She looked around as it were possible someone else could be lurking in the tiny room. "In point of fact," she said, dropping her voice, "Dr. Braithwaite had been stealing Professor Yarrow's work and passing it off as his own."

"No!" I gave her a wide-eyed look. "Professor Yarrow told you this?"

Erin suddenly looked uncomfortable, as though she'd belatedly realized she was confiding secrets to a perfect stranger. Indicating the laptop, she said, "Actually, I must finish this. It's urgent."

There was no point in pushing it and having her clam up completely. "See you later, then," I said. "I'd better get back to Dr. Wasinsky." I paused for a small, sad sigh. "I don't mind telling you, Erin, I'd love to be in your shoes, but it just didn't work out that way."

I left her with a slight, satisfied smile on her lips. She thought she was on a winner with Jack Yarrow, but I had a fair idea she was going to come an awful gutser in the near future.

⊃

This undercover stuff had turned out to be more of a strain than I'd expected. I was toey as a Roman sandal, expecting any minute I'd say something that would brand me as an imposter. It was a bonzer day, warm and sunny, so I decided to recharge my batteries by having a solitary lunch outside on the beautiful UCLA grounds.

My map indicated a North Campus Student Center. I found it without trouble and joined the students queuing for food. Eventually, I emerged into the sunlight clutching a salad in a clear plastic box, a plastic fork, several serviettes, and a carton of orange juice.

There was one dicey moment when I spied Clifford Van Horden III, strolling along while carrying on a loud cell phone conversation and checking out the female talent as he did so. Fortunately, I managed to duck behind a knot of students, and he passed by, never knowing I was there.

I found myself a spot on the grass in the nearby sculpture garden and sat cross-legged, sharing bits of my salad with a couple of entirely fearless squirrels. It would be easy to doze happily in the afternoon sun, but I had plans to make. Erin Fogarty would have to be carefully cultivated, but I was pretty sure we'd soon be best mates, and she'd be telling me how she snaffled Oscar's research for Jack Yarrow.

For the moment I thought I'd steer clear of Professor Yarrow. Ditto his wife, whose jealousy I reckoned would make her vindictive. Georgia Tapp I was going to see this afternoon. Before lunch I'd popped into her room and made an appointment to see her at three o'clock. I could see my respectful attitude had made a good impression. I hoped this would predispose her to like me, because she should be a terrif source of information.

Rube Wasinsky had set me straight on administrative assistants, and why Georgia Tapp was a very rare bird indeed. Years ago, Rube said, there'd been scads of secretaries to do the clerical stuff, but such resources vanished as government funding to universities like UCLA tightened. Now faculty members were supposed to do everything for themselves on their computers.

Professor Jack Yarrow, however, had access to private funding for a research center within the larger structure of the biology department, and he used some of this to cover the salary of his own personal administrative assistant, namely Georgia Tapp.

ᴐ

Georgia's desk was situated in a room next to Yarrow's palatial office. I put my head through the door at exactly three o'clock. "Ms. Tapp?" I raised my eyebrows tentatively. "Could you see me now?"

Georgia was on her feet, wringing her small, plump hands. Even her wispy hair seemed agitated. "I don't know whether to call the campus police or not," she hissed.

Strike me dead! Had she tumbled on to who I really was? "The cops would be a bit of an overreaction, I reckon."

She wrung her hands some more. "Listen!"

"You're a bloody bastard!" came from the adjoining office. "I'm going to expose you for what you are, Yarrow! A sniveling, pathetic arsehole who has to bloody steal my work to shore up his bloody reputation!"

I wasn't supposed to have ever met Oscar Braithwaite, so I said to Georgia, "Stone the crows! Who's that?"

Her stocky body quivering with distress, Georgia spat out, "Braithwaite. Oscar Braithwaite."

The sound of a loud thump carried through the wall. Georgia seized my wrist and wailed, "I don't know what to do. Dr. Braithwaite is capable of inflicting great bodily harm on Professor Yarrow, but Professor Yarrow will be furious if a fuss is made."

"You bloody bastard!" was followed by something indistinct from Yarrow.

"Perhaps one of us should go in and break it up," I said.

Georgia stared at me, astonished. "We can't do anything like that. They're men. They're men fighting—like primal beasts!"

Primal beasts, was it? I thought I deducted a hint of excitement underneath her chubby exterior.

A door slammed. Through Georgia's open door I saw Oscar Braithwaite's bushy head. "Bloody Yarrow! Bloody Yarrow!" he was shouting as he stamped down the hallway. His voice grew fainter, then there was another, muted slam of a door at the end of the hallway.

Georgia let out her breath in a long sigh. "He's gone," she said. I thought she sounded disappointed.

‚

There was no use trying to pump Georgia, as she was totally atwitter about the confrontation between Oscar and Yarrow, so I said I'd drop in on her tomorrow. I had a quick look around to see if I could eyeball Oscar, but he'd disappeared. I collected my car from the cavernous parking structure and drove east along Sunset Boulevard to Kendall & Creeling.

When I opened the front door, Harriet was sitting at the reception desk reading something and giggling happily to herself. When she saw me, she said, "Message from Ariana. She says to tell you she'll be back here by five-thirty."

Irritated that Melodie wasn't at her post, I said, "Where's Melodie? Don't tell me she's off on another audition."

"Not at all," said Harriet. "You'll find Melodie in the bathroom, piling on the makeup. After work she's going straight from here to the theater to try out for Quip's play." Grinning, she held up the bound pages she'd been reading. "This is the audition script. Melodie's been poring over it all day."

I took a squiz at the two-line title: *LUL (Laughter Under Luna)*

"It's a comedy?"

"Tragedy. Intensely dark tragedy." Harriet was still grinning. "I believe Quip's intention is to distill the angst of the early twenty-first century."

"But you find it funny?"

"Hilarious."

She passed the bound copy over to me. "Take a look at the front page."

Under "Characters" appeared the names: Lucy/Lucas, Ricky/Ricki, Ethel/Ethelbert, Fred/Fredricka.

Below was a Note from the Playwright, which read: "The audience will recognize iconic figures resonating in the shared group consciousness..."

"These names seem familiar," I said. "Lucy and Ricky? Ethel and Fred? It's the cast of that old TV show *I Love Lucy.*"

Harriet chuckled. "Top marks, Kylie, but things get drastically different after that. In Quip's play they're all transsexuals; their genders are changing because of pollutants in the environment. Lucy's in the process of becoming Lucas, Ricky's changing to a very feminine Ricki, Fred's on the way to Fredricka, and Ethel will be Ethelbert any day now."

"Crikey," I said, "which one has Melodie got her sights on?"

"Anything she can get." Harriet's tone was dry.

Fran and Melodie appeared, with Fran holding open what was obviously another copy of the play. Melodie was proclaiming, "Incest, incest, incest!" with great dramatic intensity.

She strode up to us and flung her arms wide. "Fratricide, filicide, matricide, patricide...um..." She dropped her arms and looked to Fran for help. "Drat! I always forget this next one."

"Parricide."

Melodie reflung her arms. "Parricide!"

"Jeez," said Harriet, "I know fratricide, matricide, and patricide respectively mean killing your brother, mother, and father. But what's filicide and what's parricide?"

Thanks to my exacting English teacher at Wollegudgerie High, I was able to enlighten her. "Parricide is killing a parent or similar authority figure. Filicide is killing a pastry."

Harriet shot me an incredulous look. "Killing a pastry? You're kidding me."

I had a bit of a giggle over filo pastry. "I am," I admitted. "That would be filocide. Filicide is killing a son or daughter."

For some reason my Aunt Millie popped into my mind. Was there an aunticide?

Meanwhile, Melodie was lifting entreating hands to the ceiling. "I embody sanguinariness," she announced, having a touch of trouble with the pronunciation. "I am slaughterous, I am—"

"Mortiferous," said Fran.

"I am mortiferous." Melodie bowed her head, then sank gracefully to her knees.

"'Strewth," I said, "the audience will need to bring their diction-aries along."

Fran, who never took kindly to even a hint of criticism where her husband was concerned, snapped, "Quip is deliberately forcing the audience to surrender to the cadence of the language without necessar-ily fully understanding what the words mean."

"I was talking to Quip this morning," said Melodie, "to get his thoughts on the essential core of Lucy-Lucas. He explained how *LUL* is deep—real deep."

"I reckon it's a bit of a challenge starting off as Lucy and ending up as Lucas," I remarked.

"For some, it would stretch their talent too thin." Melodie smiled complacently. "Fortunately, that doesn't apply to me."

"I'm sure Quip's play is very profound," I said to Fran, "but it's a bit beyond me."

For Fran, her smile was quite kindly. "Don't feel too badly, Kylie," she said. "Quip's work is a challenge to an educated American. Being an Aussie, you don't have the cultural references to decode, so yes, you're right. It is quite beyond you."

TWELVE

I sat in my office staring at the phone. I'd had a hard day, and dealing with my mother was going to be a challenge, to say the least. Perhaps I'd wait until after I'd spoken with Ariana about my experiences at UCLA. And Lonnie had left a note on my desk saying he had found something interesting, so I could postpone the call until after I'd seen him. Or I could read the bunch of brochures on garden sheds that Fran had left in a neat pile for my attention.

But then, I'd be dreading making the call, so it was preferable to get it over with. Mum had a cliché for every occasion. Right now I could hear her saying "Never put off until tomorrow what you can do today," followed by "Strike while the iron is hot." I sighed and picked up the receiver.

Before punching in the international code and the country number for Australia, I rehearsed what I would say. The plumbing emergency should be over, leaving my mum to concentrate on getting me home from the hellhole she imagined Los Angeles to be. And freeway shootings and Oscar's brush with death would provide her with fresh ammunition.

I had some responses ready. "Now, Mum," I'd say persuasively, the moment the random shootings came up, "statistics show I've got much more chance of winning the lottery than being shot on a Southern California freeway."

No, maybe that wasn't the way to go, considering my mum firmly believed she'd win the lottery any day now. "Got to be in it to win it," she always said, scanning her fistful of tickets every week.

I considered announcing I'd be more likely to be struck by lightning. But then I remembered Great Uncle Samuel, who was struck by lightning. Of course, he helped this along by standing under the tallest tree on a hill in the middle of a thunderstorm, but that wouldn't put Mum off citing him as an example of the prevalence of lightning strikes.

A jab of guilt stabbed me as I punched in the numbers. Mum loved me and wanted the best for me. Unfortunately, our ideas of what constituted the best for me did not correspond. She was determined on getting me back in Wollegudgerie to help her run the Wombat's Retreat. I was determined to stay here in L.A., learning to be a private investigator so I could pull my weight at Kendall & Creeling.

And to be totally honest, Ariana Creeling provided the most potent reason for me to stay. My heart gave a little leap of joy every time I saw her. I had to admit I was pretty well a hopeless case as far as she was concerned. Even half a chance—hell, a quarter of a chance…an eighth of a chance—that she might fall in love with me was enough reason to stick around.

Thousands of kilometers away in the outback of Australia, the pub's phone began to ring. My mother answered.

"It's Kylie, Mum. What happened with the leak in the hallway?"

"Total disaster. Danny Panopolous has ripped most of the ceiling down. There's plaster everywhere."

"But the leak's stopped, yes?"

"For the moment," she said in a deeply pessimistic tone. "Danny says half the pub's pipes are shot, and need to be replaced."

"Crikey," I said.

"And you know how Danny charges like a wounded bull. I shudder to think how much it's going to cost." I made sympathetic noises: my mum moved into attack mode. "Jack will never understand the financial side, Kylie. I've said it before, and I'll say it again—he's bloody hopeless. I desperately need you back here at the Wombat."

"Mum—"

"It's bad enough you're not at home in Australia, but to be living in Los Angeles, of all places! My blood fair curdled when I watched the news the other night. Los Angeles freeways are a shooting gallery! And that nice girl, Melodie, told about your client being mugged—in broad daylight!"

"Mum—"

"It's only a matter of time until something like that happens to you, Kylie—shot on the freeway, mugged, kidnapped, beaten, raped. How do you think I'll feel when your body's discovered?" She gave a disgusted snort. "And you say you want to stay in L.A."

"It's not like that," I protested. "Sure, you have to be careful, but it's the same in any big city."

"And that's not all," said my mother in a voice of doom. "There's the ongoing possibility of earthquakes, terrorist attacks, and severe climate change. Global warming's not a myth, you know."

She was beginning to sound more like Fran every moment. I said, "We keep disaster supplies here in the office."

"Disaster supplies? Will they protect you from killer bees? I've heard a lot about killer bees."

I managed to get in "Killer bees have been blown way out of proportion" before Mum was off again.

"I've been patient, darl—I really have, but now I see it's my duty as a mother to get you out of this situation you've got yourself into."

This was going too far. My voice icy, I said, "Decisions about my life are mine to make. I'll always listen to you, Mum, but in the long run, what I do is my affair. I'm sure I'll make mistakes, and if I do I'll pay for them. I won't whinge to you and expect sympathy."

My mother always knew when to retreat. "Live to fight another day" was how she usually put it.

There was a hurt silence at the other end of the line, then she said, "Of course you're absolutely right, Kylie. You have to make your own decisions. I can only hope that you'll eventually see it my way." A brave laugh. "I'm sure you think I'm a Nosy Parker, meddling in your affairs, but it's because I love you, darling."

"I love you too, Mum," I said dutifully.

For the next ten minutes we chatted about safer topics. My mum even managed to avoid mentioning my ex-lover, Raylene, who'd been the main reason I'd shot through to L.A. Mum's most interesting item was gossip about Aunt Millie, who had lobbed over to the States to see me and had then decided to extend her trip into a world tour.

I lived in constant dread that she would boomerang back to L.A., as she'd had such a bonzer time here, so I was fascinated to learn from Mum that Aunt Millie, who was in Britain at the moment, had taken up with some bloke called Nigel whom she'd met while on a bus tour to Bath.

"I can only hope he doesn't take advantage of my sister," said my mother.

I guffawed. This would be the equivalent of a frilled lizard taking advantage of a *Tyrannosaurus rex.*

Mum wasn't amused. "Anyone can fall for sweet-talking," she declared. "Even Millie."

"My money's on Aunt Millie. She'll eat this Nigel bloke for breakfast. I'm already feeling a bit sorry for him."

"There's no fool like an old fool," Mum declared. "Look at me."

Uh-oh! Danger signs flashed. My mother was moving into pathos. In a moment she'd be telling me that Jack hadn't turned out to be the fiancé she'd expected. And that heart-wrenching disappointment was compounded by the fact that now she had the pub to run without me and—

"Sorry, Mum, I've really got to go. I'll call you next week."

I put down the phone and let out a long sigh.

"That bad?" said Ariana at the door. My heart gave its usual joyful leap.

"Major plumbing problems at the Wombat's Retreat," I said.

Ariana knew the pressure Mum was putting on me, but I didn't want to discuss it now. Not discuss it ever, actually, because I still had the lurking thought that Ariana might want to buy me out. My fifty-one percent of Kendall & Creeling put me in a secure position. It was an advantage I never meant to lose.

Ariana came into my room and sat down across the desk from me. "Penelope Braithwaite called me this afternoon. She says she has a stalker. Some fan of her radio program who's got way out of line. She's asked me to look into it."

"It's hard to imagine anyone brave enough to stalk Pen," I said.

"She'd do them like a dinner."

"Do you want to sit in on our meeting? She'll be here in a few minutes to give me all the details."

"When I saw Pen at UCLA this morning," I said, "she didn't mention she was calling you." A dark suspicion swept over me. "This could be a setup."

"How so?" Crikey, Ariana could put volumes into one raised eyebrow.

"Pen really fancies you. She as good as said so this morning."

Ariana laughed. "I don't think so."

"Oh, come on, Ariana," I said, impatient with her. "You're a knockout, you know you are."

She sat back and gave me a long, blue look. "And you think it's likely Penelope Braithwaite will sweep me off my feet? That I'll be the equivalent of romantic cannon fodder?"

I grinned. "I reckon Pen's out of luck. You'd never allow feet-sweeping unless you wanted it to happen." I felt my smile fading. "You don't, do you?"

"Kylie—"

"Sorry," I said. "Personal question. For all I know, you and Pen Braithwaite are soul mates, made for each other."

Ariana shook her head. Before she could speak, I beat her to the punch. "You're going to say I'm one of a kind, aren't you? You've said that several times before."

"And no doubt," said Ariana drily, "I'll find myself saying it again."

Crikey, this conversation had gotten out of hand. I had a talent for putting my foot in my mouth where Ariana was concerned. I slapped a businesslike expression on my face and said in a businesslike tone, "Here's my report on what happened at UCLA today..."

ↄ

I was just finishing my report on the day's activities with a description of the violent argument Oscar had had with Jack Yarrow, when Melodie rang through to say the two Dr. Braithwaites had arrived to see Ariana.

"Two?" I said to Ariana.

She shrugged. "You'd better join us, Kylie, to even up the odds." She added with a wry smile, "And, of course, to chaperone me, if it becomes necessary."

"Blimey, you're not going to let me live that down, are you?"

"Eventually."

Ariana went to collect the Braithwaites at the front desk, I whipped off to see what Lonnie had discovered before I joined them all in Ariana's office.

Lonnie's office door was wide open. "What about Julia Roberts?" I said to him. "She can get in if your door's open."

Lonnie, hunched as usual over his computer, swung around in his chair. "She is in."

He ripped out several tissues from a box and blew his nose with a loud trumpeting noise. "When I got here this morning, Julia Roberts was in my chair. Had the devil of a time getting rid of her."

I tsk-tsked sympathetically.

Gesturing at the jumble in his room, he snarled, "And now she's back! Somewhere in here, Julia Roberts is hiding. Damn cat! I opened the door and she flew past me like a rocket and disappeared."

"Jules," I called to her, "fair go. You know very well that Lonnie's allergic. Come on out."

Lonnie tossed off a scornful laugh. "Get real, Kylie. Cats don't come when they're called. And especially not Julia Roberts. She's holed up, sneering at us both."

I could have told him what would happen next. Hearing Lonnie's disrespectful remarks about cats, Jules immediately took great pleasure in proving him wrong. There was a rustle in the middle of the room, a couple of small items shifted, and Julia Roberts emerged, tawny tail held high.

"Don't let her near me!" Lonnie implored.

Jules gave him a long, cool look, strolled over to me, paused to mark the leg of my jeans by rubbing it with her cheek and whiskers, then sauntered out the door and into the hall.

Lonnie leaped out of his chair to rush over and slam the door. He grumped back to his computer. "Damn cat. If I take any more antihistamine tablets, I'll fall unconscious at your feet."

"My cousin, Brucie, did a course of desensitization injections," I said. "They worked for his allergies. Maybe they would for you."

A look of pure horror filled Lonnie's face. "Injections?" he gasped. "I faint. I always have. All I need to see is the needle heading for my arm, and I'm gone. Out cold."

"There are nondrowsy antihistamines." Hadn't Lonnie seen the zillions of ads on teev for allergy remedies?

Lonnie dismissed my comment with a wave of his hand. "Prescription only. Too expensive." He fixed me with a calculating stare. "Kylie…"

"I'm not getting rid of Jules." I couldn't imagine living here without Julia Roberts for company.

"Get rid of is a bit harsh," said Lonnie. "I thought more relocate. Maybe Ariana could take her."

You've got Buckley's," I said.

"All right, I'll bite. What in the hell's Buckley's?"

"It comes from the Aussie saying, 'You've got two chances, Buckley's and none.' I reckon whoever Buckley was, he had the worse luck in the world, because it means you have no chance at all. A snowball in hell would be better off."

He rolled his eyes. "So Julia Roberts is staying?"

"Too right." Thinking I'd have to make Melodie promise not to open Lonnie's door, I added, "I'll do my best to make sure Jules stays out of your room."

"That's the best I can hope for," said Lonnie mournfully.

I had to get back to Ariana's office. "You left a note on my desk saying you'd found something interesting…?"

Lonnie brightened up. "I've turned up the name of an enforcer Yarrow's used before. It's possible he's the one who shoved Braithwaite into the traffic on Sunset."

"Who is it?"

"Jack Yarrow's brother-in-law. Name's Walter Easton. Known as Wally. You remember how Yarrow's divorce from his second wife,

Fenella, was as nasty as it gets? Well, this guy, Easton, is her brother."

"Yarrow was arrested for assaulting his wife, wasn't he?"

"Sure was. Fenella threw him out of the house and filed for divorce right after that." Lonnie made a face. "Dirty business. Warring attorneys. Vicious accusations on both sides. And then Fenella was assaulted again—black eyes, broken nose. But this time it was her brother. She didn't press charges, said it was a family argument."

"You think Jack Yarrow was responsible for this attack?"

"Looks that way. Easton and Yarrow have remained thick as thieves. When Yarrow took Winona Worsack as his third wife, he married into a very wealthy family. I don't think it's a coincidence that once Yarrow had access to money, he set Wally Easton up in business, financing him in Wally's Strength & Health Club in Burbank. There've been rumors that Easton has been dealing in illegal steroids and the like, but he's never been convicted."

Lonnie gave me a printout detailing Wally Easton's career, and I took it along with me to Ariana's office, thinking I'd check with Oscar and Pen to see if either one was familiar with Yarrow's brother-in-law.

The moment I entered the office, I had an I-told-you-so moment. Oscar was his usual hairy, untidy self, but Pen...

Pen was a substantial vision in a bright-turquoise outfit, which I thought the exact same shade as her little sports car. In Ariana's black-and-white room, she positively glowed. Her humongous sandals had been replaced with high heels. Her burnished hair was up, she wore dangling earrings, also turquoise, and a matching bracelet. She'd clearly taken some time applying makeup. Most alarming of all, she was smiling fondly at Ariana.

My gaze locked with Ariana's. I raised my eyebrows fractionally. She sent me a you-were-right resigned smile.

"Pen," I said, "you're looking bonzer. Got a big date tonight?"

"I can only hope," said Pen, grinning meaningfully at Ariana. "I can only hope."

THIRTEEN

"Bloody stalker," snarled Oscar Braithwaite. "When I catch him I'll thrash him within an inch of his life."

With an obvious effort, Pen switched her attention from Ariana to her brother. Clearly irate, she said, "Oscar, how many times have I told you? Don't get involved. Leave it to the professionals."

Oscar glowered at her through a curtain of hair. "A good beating—that's what the bastard needs."

Pen gave an irritated sigh. "Honestly," she said to Ariana and me, "Oscar can be a pain, as you can see. He's been this way since we were kids, playing superprotective brother." She snorted. "As though I've ever needed much protection!"

"Stalkers are different," Oscar declared. "They're dangerous fanatics—stop at nothing."

"Precisely why we're here," said Pen. "Anyone who has an advice program like mine gets their share of obsessive fans, but this one's something else. For the past two months, he's left written messages everywhere I go, even in my university office. And of course, there's the constant delivery of flowers. I've got to the point that I shudder every time I see a florist's van."

"You've kept these notes?" Ariana asked.

Pen's mouth twisted with distaste. "Kept the notes? No way. I barely scan them before they hit the trash."

"Please keep any you get from now on and try not to handle them too much."

"All right, I'll do that, but I guarantee there won't be fingerprints," said Pen. "This one's too smart. For example, he uses a different florist every time. I tried a spot of detective work myself, and called a couple of florists to find out who'd ordered the flowers. Got nowhere."

Ariana's signet ring flashed as she picked up a ballpoint—black, of course. "I'd like the name of any florist you remember delivering flowers to you."

After Pen had named the three she recalled, Ariana said, "What about telephone calls?"

"I may have spoken to him. I'm not sure. Callers to my radio show are screened, so the real crazies never get through to me. As an additional safeguard, there's a ten-second delay on the broadcast, so if necessary I can cut the person off before anything objectionable goes to air. Lately, I've had a few odd calls that seem to be from the same man. He isn't initially screened out because he sounds a reasonable human being until he gets me on the line."

"What does he say?" Ariana asked.

Pen grimaced. "Like the notes, extreme violence. Sexual sadism. Nothing I haven't heard before, but it's different when it's directed at me, personally."

"What would you expect?" demanded Oscar, bouncing in his seat. "You openly encourage grubby little people to sprout grubby little stories about their bodily functions."

"Oscar has a few hangups," said Pen, smiling indulgently at her brother.

I braced myself for an explosion, but Oscar merely spluttered ineffectually and then subsided.

"What about calls to your home phone?" said Ariana.

"Nothing so far. The number's unlisted."

"That's no protection against someone determined to get to you. Let an answering machine pick up all your calls from now on."

Pen frowned. "So you think he's going to start pestering me on my home phone?"

"I'm surprised he hasn't already," Ariana remarked.

Curious, I asked, "How do you know it's a man? Could the calls to the radio station be made by a woman disguising her voice?"

Pen shifted her glance to me. "Do women stalk? I would have thought they'd have better things to do with their time."

"Women stalk," said Ariana. "And they can be just as dangerous. Is there anything to indicate this person could be someone with whom you had a prior relationship?"

Pen grinned. "No way. I leave my lovers of both sexes fully satisfied."

Ariana's serious expression didn't change. "A large proportion of stalkers have had some sort of intimate relationship with their victims."

Affronted, Pen declared, "I'm not a victim—and never will be!"

"If you're being stalked, you're the victim of a crime," said Ariana. "Have you considered going to the police?"

"Bloody cops," said Oscar. "Steer clear of them, I say."

Pen smiled warmly at Ariana. "First, let's see what you come up with, Ariana."

Ariana didn't smile back. "I'll give you a printed list of precautionary steps to take. As I'll be in Sacramento tomorrow and Friday, I suggest Bob Verritt takes over your case. He's a very experienced investigator and well-versed in problems like yours."

"Sacramento?" Pen seemed disappointed, but then her spirits visibly lightened. "But you're free this evening—"

"I'm afraid not. I have a flight first thing in the morning, so I intend to have an early night."

Pen beamed. "What a coincidence. I had in mind an early night too."

Ariana's blue eyes narrowed. My cue to step in and change the subject. "Do either of you know a bloke called Wally Easton? There's a possibility he was the one who sent Oscar hurtling into the traffic."

"You know who the bugger is?" said Oscar. "Show me."

I displayed two photos of Wally Easton, which Lonnie had taken from the Web site for Wally's Strength & Health Club. One had him in a minuscule bathing costume, striking a bodybuilding pose. His bulging muscles glistened with oil, and his face wore an expression of arrogant superiority. The second photo, head and shoulders, showed the same egotistical conceit. He had an impressive physique, if you liked that sort of overdeveloped body, but he wasn't handsome. A small head perched on a thick neck. His mouth was too close to his nose, and his eyes were small and beady. He'd shaved his skull, and it too glistened with oil.

Pen shook her head. "Total stranger. Looks terminally stupid."

Oscar, who'd examined each photograph carefully, said, "I've seen him somewhere, and not long ago. Can't remember when or where. Who is he?"

"Professor Yarrow's brother-in-law. At least he was. He's Yarrow's second wife's brother." I went on to give the details Lonnie had found, including how Easton had escaped being charged with bashing his own sister.

"Hit a woman?" said Oscar. "The bastard should be given a taste of his own medicine."

"Not by you, Oscar," said Pen, looking grim. "If you see this Wally Easton again, keep away from him."

Oscar rumbled incoherently.

Apparently able to translate, Pen snapped, "Have you got a death wish? Look at those muscles. He'd tear you limb from limb."

Oscar moved his shoulders irritably, and mumbled something in a sulky tone.

Pen's reddening face indicated there was about to be a nasty scene, but fortunately Ariana smoothly interposed with, "To get back to the matter of your stalker, shall I call Bob Verritt in so you can brief him?"

"That won't be necessary," said Pen. "Kylie here and I are great mates already, aren't we? She can hold the fort until you get back."

"But I'm at UCLA all day," I pointed out.

"Not a problem. So far, my stalker's only writing notes and sending flowers and maybe calling me on my radio show…" She jabbed a finger in my direction. "That's it! I'm on air Saturday night. You can sit in, see the setup, and if he calls in, hear him in action."

I glanced at Ariana. "What do you think?"

"It could be useful, but it's up to you."

I had the weekend free, as Chantelle was going to be away on a company retreat. "Good-oh," I said to Pen. "You're on."

With a faintly lascivious smile, Pen offered me dinner before her show and seemed only marginally disappointed when I declined. We made arrangements to meet at the radio station, then Pen and the sullen Oscar departed.

I saw them out to the parking lot, and was amused to see I'd been right—Pen's clothes were the exact turquoise shade as her little Mazda. Oscar grunted when I said goodbye. Pen smiled cheerily. "Until Saturday!"

I went back to Ariana's stark office to find her putting papers into her briefcase. Usually, we had a staff meeting first thing on Monday morning to discuss our workloads for the week, but last Monday the initial interview with Oscar Braithwaite had intervened, so I hadn't known Ariana was going to be out of town.

"What are you doing in Sacramento?" I asked, already feeling the loss of her presence, which was ridiculous, because I'd be at UCLA most of Thursday and Friday anyway and I rarely saw her on Saturdays or Sundays.

"Deposition in a blackmail case, and while I'm there I'll follow up on a witness in a case of political corruption Bob's investigating."

Ariana's phone rang. It was Melodie to say Chantelle was calling me. "United Flair's taking everyone to Big Sur for the weekend," said Melodie, "that's a real nice place. Chantelle has all the luck."

I told Melodie I'd take the call in my office. Before I left Ariana, I said, "Where's Big Sur?"

"Big Sur? It's on the coastal highway about two hundred miles north of here. It has the most beautiful scenery."

There was something in her voice that made me ask, "Have you stayed there?"

Her face closed. Turning back to her briefcase she said, "Yes, many times."

Crikey, I'd touched a nerve. I trotted down to my office to pump Chantelle about Big Sur.

"Oh, it's gorgeous," she said. "A wild rocky coast and loads of great big trees. The lodge where we're having our company retreat is right next to a national park. We've got scuba diving and hikes and stuff like that lined up for when we're not getting in touch with our inner animals."

97

Chantelle had mentioned this before. Over the weekend everyone at United Flair, from the talent agents right through to people in the mail room, would join in mind games designed to help each person could get in touch with his or her inner animal. This was supposed to markedly improve relationships in the workplace, although I couldn't quite see how.

"What if you turn out to be a rattlesnake, and your boss a timid little mouse?" I asked. "Or maybe you're a hummingbird, and your boss is a crocodile. One snap and you're gone."

"I've already decided what I'm going to be," Chantelle announced. "A big cat. A black panther, to be precise."

"You're choosing what you want to be beforehand? Aren't you supposed to go through all these tests and exercises to find out what you are?"

Chantelle gave one of her warm, dusky chuckles. "Honey," she said, "no way am I going to be some creepy, second-rate animal. I'll play along with everything and voilà!—discover I'm a big cat at just the right moment."

"Black panther does suit you," I conceded, thinking of her sleek, dark skin.

"Keep that thought," she purred.

I hung up the phone, smiling. Then I thought about Big Sur and Ariana's reaction, and my smile went south. The place must mean something special to her. Perhaps it had to do with Natalie Ives.

To keep my mind on business, I took out my trusty copy of *Private Investigation: The Complete Handbook* and turned to the chapter titled "Stalking the Stalker." I discovered that stalkers could be divided into three types: former intimate partners, delusional individuals, and avengers.

I saw why Ariana had asked Pen if her stalker could be someone she'd had an intimate relationship with, as well over half of stalkers fell into this category. Intimate stalkers, I read, refuse to believe a relationship is over, no matter what the object of their obsession says or does. There is no reasoning with them. They hear what they want to hear, twisting outright rejection into a declaration of love.

The second type, delusional stalkers, my handbook pointed out, were quite different. Generally they had had no personal contact with their victims. Unable to form real, rewarding relationships themselves, they opted for imaginary ones, almost always with celebrities or other people of much higher status than they were. Many stalkers in this category were mentally ill, often suffering from erotomania, where they were totally convinced the victim fervently adored and desired them. Most were convinced their loved one was beaming them hidden messages, encoded in public statements.

The third type of stalker was the avenger. This was a person who had become furiously angry with someone because of a real or imagined slight. Politicians, judges, bosses, and colleagues at work were often victims of these stalkers, who saw themselves as justified in getting even, and having revenge upon those who had enraged them.

I'd just turned the page to the section on advice to give stalking victims, when there was a knock at the door, and Fran waltzed in, her expression determined.

"Had time to look at the garden sheds?" she asked, staring pointedly at the untouched pile of brochures she'd left for me to read.

"Not yet. Sorry." I thought of my conversation with Fran at the reception desk a little earlier, and felt a dash of determination myself. "Please close the door and sit down," I said, as cool as Ariana. "There's something we need to discuss."

Fran seemed puzzled. "Apart from the sheds—and you haven't even looked at anything yet—what is there to discuss?"

I'd had enough of this sheila. "Do I have to fight you every centimeter? Please shut the door and sit down."

Fran complied with bad grace. "OK," she said, glaring at me. "Door closed and I'm sitting."

I took a deep breath, not quite sure how to begin. I'd just play it by ear and see what happened. "If you were picked up and plunked in the middle of Wollegudgerie, my hometown, you'd be a fish out of water."

Fran squinted belligerently at me. "So?"

"So you wouldn't like it if Aussies mocked and scorned you because you didn't understand everything about the place."

Fran's china-doll features were showing a glimmer of understanding. "So?" she said, less emphatically.

"So I've had it with you," I said, quite calmly. "I'm still a stranger here, and I'm trying to learn the ropes as fast as I can. Sure, I don't understand every cultural reference, but you wouldn't either if you were in Oz."

I expected an argument, but Fran was looking at me with something close to respect—an unaccustomed experience for me.

"OK, Kylie, I'll cut you some slack."

"Meaning you'll give me a fair go?"

"I guess that's what I mean." She gave me a faint smile.

Now I was at a loss for what to say. I'd been ready for a donnybrook, and Fran agreeing with me took the wind right out of my sails.

"Right-oh," I said. "Good."

"That's it?"

"That's it."

Fran paused at the door. "We must have these little chats more often." Her tone was sardonic.

She was gone before I could have the last word. Wouldn't it rot your socks?

FOURTEEN

Thursday and Friday I worked flat out at UCLA, having been co-opted by Professor Yarrow to help the committee running the Global Marsupial Symposium. Any worries I had that someone would catch me out about the research paper I was supposedly writing under Rube Wasinsky's supervision receded, as everyone was totally concentrated on the myriad organizational demands created by such a prestigious international conference.

I checked list after list of attendees to ensure no one would be insulted by receiving a misspelled name tag. This task was more demanding than it sounded, as many countries were represented and so many people had, for English speakers like me, challenging names. Then I was set troubleshooting problems that had occurred with catering for all the different cultures. I was kept so busy that I hardly had time to say hello to Rube or work on becoming friends with Erin Fogarty so that I could pump her some more about the quokka research Oscar had said she'd stolen to give to Jack Yarrow.

On Thursday I did manage to fit in my appointment with Georgia Tapp, Yarrow's administrative assistant. We chatted for a while about how wonderful the professor was, how his keen, incisive mind and forceful personality had elevated the Global Marsupial Symposium to the must-go event in the scientific world. Then her cheerful, dimpled face grew grim. "Such great success breeds envy. Little people try to drag the professor down."

"You mean Dr. Braithwaite?"

"That creature! You heard him yesterday in his unwarranted,

intemperate attack upon Professor Yarrow, a man whose boots he's not fit to shine!"

"Awful," I murmured.

"Something has to be done," said Georgia Tapp. "Braithwaite has to be stopped before he goes too far."

I tried a puzzled but attentive expression. It worked.

"Can you imagine?" Georgia snarled. "He's claiming Professor Yarrow has stolen his quokka research." She took a few agitated breaths. "As if Professor Yarrow would need to pass other's work off as his own!"

I shook my head. "Hard to believe."

"The truth is—" Georgia broke off to lean forward conspiratorially. "The truth is, we've learned Braithwaite intends to attack Professor Yarrow's credibility in front of an audience of the greatest marsupial experts in the world."

"Surely they won't believe him," I said. "I mean, Professor Yarrow is such an eminent authority."

"Mud can stick," she declared darkly. "That's why something has to be done."

What this something might be I was not to discover, as Jack Yarrow himself appeared at her office door. "Kylie?" he said with rather chilly surprise. "I thought you were helping with the symposium arrangements."

"Sorry, Prof. Stopped to chat. Won't do it again."

"Professor," said Yarrow and Georgia in unison.

"Sorry again." I smiled sweetly at Yarrow, who was blocking my exit by standing in the doorway. "It's like you said before, I've got that annoying Aussie tendency to use diminutives."

He didn't look amused, but he did manage to press himself against me as I squeezed past him. Yerks!

⊃

By late Friday afternoon I was more than glad to say goodbye to the biology department and head for home. I reached Kendall & Creeling, parked my car, and stopped, as I often did, to admire the courtyard at the front of the building. Its little terra-cotta fountain burbled happily to itself. I'd recently bought a selection of tree ferns to create shade in one corner, and I had my eye on a stone bench I'd seen in one of the zillion catalogs that constantly arrived in the mail. Melodie, who was the catalog queen, was always poring over one or the other and announcing she'd found something she just must have.

Melodie herself appeared, traipsing listlessly across the red terra-cotta tiles of the courtyard in the direction of the parking area.

"Oh, hello," she said, shoulders drooping. "I left your messages on your desk."

"Whatever's the matter?"

Melodie dumped her voluminous makeup bag on the ground. "Ashlee." Her voice was bitter. "The hush-up didn't work. Ashlee found out Quip is auditioning for *LUL* all this week." She sighed. "Ashlee says she'll be at tonight's auditions."

"There was a leak in the receptionist network?"

Melodie put heart and soul into a dark scowl. "If I find out who…"

"It'll be curtains? She'll be cast into receptionist outer darkness? Much gnashing of teeth?"

Melodie zapped me with a look. "You can joke, Kylie, but this is serious. Ashlee's heart is set on playing Lucy/Lucas, would you believe? That's my role. I told Quip I was prepared to dye my hair red so I could fully realize the very essence of a redheaded character."

"That makes sense," I said encouragingly. "As a blond, you only know the essence of blondness, like I know the essence of dark brown."

Melodie gave me a very suspicious look. I maintained a bland expression. "Good luck," I said. "I can't imagine Ashlee's got a chance, with you in the running."

She brightened. "It's true Ashlee can't act, but…" Melodie trailed off as gloom took over again.

"What?" I said.

"It isn't fair," Melodie snapped. "Ashlee's a natural redhead."

"Like Fran."

Frowning, Melodie said, "Why are you mentioning Fran? She isn't trying out for the part." A look of alarm spread over her face. "Omigod!

Fran left early today. And I did hear her reading lines to Lonnie in the kitchen. You don't think—"

"Surely Fran would have told you?"

Melodie snatched up her makeup bag. "Gotta go," she said, putting her ankles at risk as she broke into a near run in her extremely high heels.

Melodie's had been the only other car in the parking area, so I knew I was alone in the building except for Julia Roberts. She was waiting for me just inside the front door. I'd been held up at UCLA last night, and Jules had been served her dinner half an hour late. This, she had made plain, was unacceptable. Tonight, the moment she set eyes on me, Jules began lobbying for sustenance. This was more to make a point than to be sure she got fed on time, because she knew that when I was in residence, I was pretty well putty in her paws.

I locked the door, soothed Jules by giving her a quick groom—for a short-haired cat, it was amazing how much she managed to shed—then went to check my messages.

Mum had called to say she'd seen another L.A. freeway shooting on the news, and that I was not, under any circumstances, to take my life in my hands and drive on freeways. Melodie had scrawled on the bottom of the message: "Your mom was real upset."

Lonnie had left a note to advise me he'd installed a pinhole-lens camera linked to a time-lapse VCR at Pen Braithwaite's apartment. The VCR was set to record an image every second, which would catch anyone approaching the front door of the apartment. Like Melodie, Lonnie had added something. In his case it was a smiley face and the words: "Dr. Penny! Cool!"

Julia Roberts had followed me into my office. I was telling her we could head to the kitchen for her tucker when I heard someone at the front door. Yerks! I was nowhere near my usual protective weapon, a golf club I kept behind my bedroom door.

"Kylie? It's me, Ariana."

My heart gave a delighted jump. I hadn't expected to see Ariana until Monday. I put on a casual expression and went to meet her.

Ariana looked tired. "I'm just calling in to pick up my messages," she said, smothering a yawn. "I'm beat. My plane was delayed two hours, and then we had a rough flight. I hoped to pick up Gussie, but we landed too late for me to make it to the Castle in time."

"The castle?"

Ariana smiled. "Believe it or not, the name of the boarding kennels is Canine Castle. The latest in luxury accommodations for dogs. Gussie seems to enjoy herself there."

Carefully nonchalant, I said, "So there's no one at home waiting for you to arrive?"

"The odd potted plant might pine for my company," said Ariana lightly.

"Stay and have dinner with me." When she seemed about to demur, I added, "Oh, come on, Ariana. There's a local Thai restaurant I've got to know well. Beaut tucker. I can call an order in, and half an hour, tops, it'll be ready to pick up." Before she could say no, I went on, "I'll get the menu. Have a look at it and see what you think."

"Thanks, but I was dreaming of a hot shower and getting into something comfortable. I'll take a rain check, OK?"

"You can have a shower here, while I order. And I'm sure you've got a change of clothes in your luggage. Please. I'd really like the company."

"You have Julia Roberts," said Ariana, indicating Jules, who had chosen this moment to stalk up to us, her ears slanted in a frown. She sat down and glared at me. After all her efforts, I still hadn't provided her dinner on schedule.

"She's lovely," I said, "but just a touch self-centered. Basically, it's Jules, Jules, Jules. I don't get a look-in." I sloped my eyebrows the wrong way and looked hopefully at Ariana.

"I'm too tired to resist," Ariana said with a half laugh. "Where's the menu?"

⊃

The Kendall & Creeling Building had originally been a private home, so there were two proper bathrooms. The one the staff used had a bathtub with a showerhead and, of course, a toilet. Mine, off my bed-

105

room, was smaller, but it had a frosted glass shower recess. I'd always considered it dangerous to clamber into a slippery bathtub to have a shower and said so to Ariana. "It's much safer to use my bathroom."

"I'll use the office one," she said, a little too emphatically.

"Are you thinking I'm going to put the hard word on you?" I asked. When she raised one eyebrow fractionally, I translated, although I was certain she knew exactly what I meant. "Make a pass at you, come on to you—whatever it is you Americans say."

"Kylie—"

"Because I won't. Promise."

And I meant it. No way was I going to ruin things between us. I had to admit I'd almost blown it a few weeks back, when I'd said too much, but since then I'd played it cool, and things were again back on an even keel.

"OK." Ariana picked up her things and headed for the staff bathroom. I called the Thai restaurant with our order, then served Julia Roberts with grilled turkey, one of her favorites. Actually, she had a healthy appetite, so pretty well every different dinner was a favorite.

I'd picked up my keys to collect our order when Ariana came into the kitchen barefoot and wearing faded blue jeans and a black T-shirt. "You didn't have black jeans?" I asked, grinning.

"Apparently not," she said drily. "Do you want me to come with you?"

"No, stay here and keep Jules company."

"Then let me pay."

"I asked you to dinner, so it's my shout."

I left her with Jules watching TV in the kitchen and skipped out to my car. I reminded myself not to get too chuffed about having persuaded Ariana to share a meal with me. It was no big deal. She'd eat, stay for a few polite minutes more, then go off to her Hollywood Hills home with its stunning views…and maybe, its memories.

Memories. What was it that made her so sad? Had someone she cared for died? Or was it a love story that had ended badly? But how could anyone fall out of love with Ariana? I suspected I'd find it impossible.

On autopilot, I drove the kilometer or so to the Thai restaurant, rehearsing what I'd say to Ariana when I got back. Maybe she would let her hair down and talk about herself…. Oh, that was likely—as likely as me spotting a flock of pink pigs flying along Sunset Boulevard.

Miraculously, I snaffled a parking spot after driving around the block only once, chatted with the sweet little daughter of the Thai family who owned the shop, collected my order, and, feeling supercheerful, left a large tip. Before starting my car, I hesitated. Should I pick up a bottle of wine to have with our food? Would it look as though I had an ulterior motive? That I was plying her with alcohol to have my way with her?

My way with her: I had to grin at the old-fashioned phrase. I resolutely ignored a frisson of desire. I'd promised, hadn't I? So, no wine. No hidden agenda. Just a pleasant meal together.

Speeding back to Ariana, I resolved to be a relaxed, agreeable dinner companion. As I drove through our gate, I glanced at our names: Kendall & Creeling. Our business relationship: crash-hot if it could be our personal relationship too. I sternly reminded myself not to be impetuous. My mother had often pointed out how often I got myself in hot water because I acted without first thinking it through. Tonight I would be caution personified.

I found Ariana perched on a high stool in the kitchen, Julia Roberts rather precariously situated on her lap. "Gussie will smell Jules on your clothes," I said, dumping the plastic bag containing our dinner on the counter.

"She won't mind. Gussie loves cats. She's very respectful, probably because she had a cat of her own for quite a few years: Priscilla."

I was eager to glean any personal details. "What happened to Priscilla?" I asked.

"She was nineteen," said Ariana, "so I believe one can say old age happened to Priscilla."

"You had her from a kitten?"

Ariana smiled. "She was an incredibly soft, furry little ball of energy."

I would have kept this conversation going, just to see where it would lead, but Ariana gently deposited Julia Roberts on the floor and headed for the food.

We sat companionably across from each other at the kitchen bench, open containers of many different Thai delicacies between us. I particularly liked that about Thai food—the mixture of many flavors to compliment and contrast. As she served herself, I noticed she'd removed her signet ring.

We didn't talk much, just concentrated on eating. Afterward, over coffee (Ariana) and tea (me), I brought Ariana up to speed on what had been happening while she'd been away in Sacramento. "What with the Global Marsupial Symposium starting on Thursday next week, everyone in the biology department is flat out like a lizard drinking," I said, "so I haven't had much chance to chat up Erin Fogarty about Oscar's quokka research. Monday morning, first thing, I'm going to turn on the charm full bore."

"Difficult to see how she can resist," said Ariana in a dry tone.

I gave her a cheeky grin. "End of the day, I practically guarantee that I'll be her second best friend."

"I don't doubt it. But why aim so low? Why not be Erin Fogarty's first best friend?"

Crikey, I loved her cool, astringent wit. More than that, I loved her. "You know I said I wasn't going to put the hard word on you?"

Ariana looked at me mutely, her eyes so blue they glowed.

I took a deep breath. "I lied. I want you to stay the night. Here. With me."

She shook her head. "Bad idea."

"Be a devil, Ariana. Throw caution to the winds."

Her mouth quirked, just a little. "It's not in my character." She slid off the kitchen stool. "Kylie, this isn't going to work. There are so many things you don't know."

"Then tell me."

"I can't."

"Or won't?"

"Both."

"Blimey," I said, "you don't make things easy, do you?" We were standing toe-to-toe. I leaned forward and kissed her wonderful mouth. Her heart was beating hard against me. "Come to bed."

She stood within the circle of my arms, unresisting, her head bent. Barefoot, she was a bit shorter than me, but I'd reckon more than my match. I could feel the taut muscles in her back, sense the tensile strength of her.

Ariana's breath had quickened; there was a faint tremor in her body. I knew she desired me—or desired someone—to hold her, make love to her. Perhaps any warm body would do. Perhaps she saw the image of someone else when she looked at me. Perhaps…

She looked up. "All right," she said. "I'll stay."

"Thank you."

"Thank you?"

I felt myself blushing. "I didn't expect you to agree," I added hastily, "and I'm really chuffed you have, Ariana. You won't change your mind, will you?"

Suddenly, she looked terribly sad. "No," she said, "I won't change my mind. I should—but I won't."

I couldn't help feeling a bit hurt. At least she could pretend a degree of enthusiasm. "Stone the crows," I said, "that's a bit less than a ringing endorsement for my company. I mean, I'm not expecting for you to fall over yourself, but…"

A small smile touched the corners of her mouth. "Kylie, you're one of a kind," she said. "You really are."

ↄ

I left her sitting on my bed communing with Julia Roberts, and went to have a shower myself, but not before I said to Ariana, "You won't choof off the moment I get under the shower, will you?"

"I guess that means skip out on you. I'm exhausted, Kylie. I'm too tired to even think about getting up and leaving."

She wasn't kidding. Sparkling clean, wrapped in a terry toweling robe, I bounded out of the bathroom to find Julia Roberts and Ariana curled up on my bed, both sound asleep.

Still in her jeans and T-shirt, her blond hair spread across the pillow, she slept like a child, relaxed and vulnerable. I didn't want to disturb her, so I turned out the light and, still wrapped in my robe, eased myself onto the bed beside her. Julia Roberts sighed, leaped gracefully to the floor, and left us. Three, apparently, was a crowd.

I may have dozed a little, but the delight of having Ariana's sleeping self beside me kept me pretty much alert. Her breathing was slow and easy. There was enough reflected light in the room for me to discern her unguarded face. I thought there was a real possibility my heart would melt with tenderness.

Ages passed. The world spun on its axis, unheeding. She lay within the crook of my arm. I didn't wish for morning, even though my arm had a severe case of pins and needles. I heard the cadence of her breathing change, and realized she was awake. After a few moments, she said, "Hi."

"G'day."

In the silence, I was conscious of the faint rumble of traffic on Sunset Boulevard. I eased my arm out from under her and flexed my fingers. "Pins and needles," I said. "You're heavier than you look."

Ariana gave a soft laugh.

"Crikey," I said, "that wasn't very romantic, was it?"

"Not very." Her voice was husky.

Leaning on my elbow, I looked down at Ariana's face. In the near darkness the devastating blueness of her eyes was masked. My heart was hammering so hard I thought she must hear it. Perhaps she did. She slid her hand under my robe, encircled my shoulders, and pulled me down into a kiss, slow and deep.

The touch of her clothes against my bare skin was intoxicating. I felt her reach for her waistband. "Don't undress, Ariana. Not yet."

She made a soft, languorous sound as I ran my fingers down the seam of her jeans. I pushed up her T-shirt, kissed her stomach, stroked her nipples with my tongue.

"Kylie," she said.

My name in her mouth ignited such longing, such passion that I heard myself moan. I'd reached the zenith. Afire, I knew I couldn't feel more, couldn't desire more. Then Ariana touched me, and I found I'd only brushed the edges of ecstasy. I muffled my cries against her throat. Ariana—cool, controlled Ariana—had vanished in an incendiary flash. She ripped the T-shirt over her head and tossed it aside. She lifted her hips as I peeled her jeans down, quivered as I tasted her.

She was lightning; she was quicksilver; she was my Ariana.

FIFTEEN

After making love with Ariana, anything else was set to be an anti-climax. On Saturday evening I arrived at the radio station at the appointed time. I'd been quite looking forward to sitting in the studio watching Pen, as Dr. Penny, dispensing advice to callers, but now my thoughts were fixed on something far more disturbing—and exciting.

As I parked my car in the lot beside the khaki-colored building that had seen better times, I reminded myself I had to collect a compilation of the suspicious calls that Pen had had made up from the master recordings of her show. My name had been given to security, so after I'd been thoroughly checked to make sure I was who I said I was and then provided with a badge reading VISITOR, Pen was summoned to collect me from the reception area.

Bubbling with enthusiasm, she punched the button to summon the lift at least ten times. "That Lonnie of yours, he's quite a ladies' man," she said. "Sexy as all get-out."

"Lonnie?" Chubby, dimpled Lonnie—sexy? Pen had to be referring to someone else.

"He did a great job installing the pinhole camera," Pen continued. "And he stayed for quite a while. We found we had so much in common."

I visualized Lonnie next to the Amazonian Pen Braithwaite. He was shorter than me, so he'd probably be about her breast level. And Lonnie was a total technology freak, who didn't seem to have a private life at all. What could he and Pen possibly have in common?

"Now, don't tell Rube," said Pen, smiling girlishly at me. "He can get

112

quite jealous at times, although we do have an open relationship."

"There's nothing to tell Rube," I pointed out. "Lonnie just installed a surveillance unit for you."

Pen's smile widened. She gave me an affectionate, one-armed squeeze that pushed most of the air out of my lungs. "Little you know!" she said, following this with a hoot of laughter.

Could she mean it? Lonnie had written: "Dr. Penny! Cool!" on the bottom of his note to me about the camera installation. But, Lonnie and Pen Braithwaite? Quite unexpected pictures danced in front of my eyes.

"I hope you'll be very happy together," I declared.

"Speaking of happy," said Pen, peering closely at me, "you look positively sated, Kylie. Some wonderfully sensual experience?"

I knew I was blushing. "Fair," I said, offhand. "Nothing to write home to Mum about."

And that was true. My mum would never hear a word about my night with Ariana.

Thankfully at this moment the lift arrived with a tired wheeze, and Pen swept me into it. She jabbed the floor number multiple times. "Come on," she said, "Come on!" The lift doors creaked arthritically closed.

"Bloody elevators," said Pen. "Got stuck in this one the other day. And I was by myself, worse luck. Now, if it gives up the ghost right now, it'll be you and me, Kylie, all alone. What do you say to that?"

"Help?"

"Love it," said Pen, chuckling, "that Aussie sense of humor."

Heeding my urgent prayer, the lift opened on the correct floor. "Better luck next time, eh?" said Pen, striding in the direction of double doors with an illuminated ON AIR sign.

We passed a window through which I could see a bloke at a console speaking animatedly into a microphone, although we could hear nothing until we entered the control room, where his voice was fed through speakers. He was giving news headlines: high-speed police pursuit of a carjacked SUV, influence peddling scandal in City Hall, gang-related shootout in one of the poorer L.A. areas, top movie star checks into upscale substance abuse clinic.

"Same old, same old," said Pen.

In quick succession, she introduced me to several preoccupied peo-ple, each of whom said. "Hi," then went straight back to preparing for the coming program. One called Roger seemed to be in charge. Then I was bundled into a cramped studio, seated in a high-backed leather chair, and fitted with cumbersome earphones. "Can you hear me?" boomed in my ears. I gestured to the sound engineer to indicate I could.

Then there was a lull in proceedings. Through the window between the control room and the studio, I could see Pen waving her hands around as she spoke to a diminutive woman who for some reason reminded me of an aristocratic whippet. If she'd been larger, I reflect-ed, it'd have been a greyhound.

With nothing to distract me, my thoughts boomeranged back to Ariana. This morning we'd breakfasted together, and Ariana had been quiet but not cold. If anything, she'd been pensive, even sad. I'd silently admonished myself not to say too much. Any declaration of love, for example, was definitely not on the schedule. Both of us scrupulously avoided discussing our night together, and I managed not to impul-sively blurt anything out about undying devotion over my porridge.

The rot had set in when I'd walked Ariana to her dark-blue BMW. She said a casual goodbye, slid into the driver's seat, shut the door, started the engine.

I tapped gently on her window. She slid it down and gazed inquir-ingly at me. "Something you forgot?"

"To tell you that I love you."

Ariana looked away. "Don't say that, please."

"Why not? It's true."

"Please."

"Right-oh," I'd said, "but it won't make any difference. I'll still love you."

We hadn't exchanged another word. I'd stepped back, and she'd put the car in gear and driven away.

Pen broke into my thoughts by barging through the studio door.

The room seemed suddenly smaller. In the space of a couple minutes, she'd dumped the compilation of questionable calls in my lap, flung herself into a chair opposite mine, slapped down a bunch of typed pages, whacked on her earphones, fiddled with switches, and adjusted the hanging microphone to her liking. This was followed by a sound-level check.

All this accomplished, she leaned back and grinned at me. "If the guy calls, and I'm betting he will, Roger's on the ten-second delay, and the program will go to station identification while I keep him talking."

Roger came through the earphones to say it was sixty seconds to airtime.

"Have you listened to my program before?" Pen asked me.

I had to admit I'd missed that pleasure.

Pen chortled. "Be ready to be surprised."

I said I would be.

"Emily screens the calls," said Pen, indicating the whippet woman, who was seated on the other side of the dividing window, earphones dominating her narrow head. "She's got a talent for voices, and will recognize Creepy Guy—that's what we've taken to calling him—if he's on the line. I've told her to put him through like a regular caller." She rubbed her hands together. "Creepy's starting to be a bit of a challenge. I always like a challenge."

"No, you don't," I said, having read much more about stalking and stalkers since last we'd talked. "True stalkers are much more than a challenge. They're unhinged, unpredictable individuals who can go from being a mere nuisance to becoming a murderous threat."

Pen seemed ready to argue, but I went on, "Did you read through the list of preliminary steps that Ariana gave you?"

She waved a dismissive hand. "All just common sense. Besides, being a celebrity of sorts, I've already got more than half of them in place."

The basic safety precautions to take when being stalked were, as Pen said, common sense: block your address at the DMV and voter registration; get a post office box for mail; screen all calls with an answering machine; get an additional, unlisted number and only give it to family and very close friends; never accept delivery of a package unless you personally ordered the item; shred all receipts and statements; keep a cell phone by your side at all times, even inside your home, because a stalker can cut telephone wires; get a watchdog; install a security system including video surveillance of entry points; be aware of exactly where the nearest police station is; establish where twenty-four-hour stores are situated; inform neighbors, coworkers, and friends that you are being stalked so they won't innocently provide information; take a class in self-defense; consider changing your address.

I'd opened my mouth to emphasize that taking a stalker for granted had been a fatal mistake for some victims when a voice in our earphones started the countdown. The program was about to go to air. The theme music, I found, was the old Cole Porter song "Anything Goes." I had a feeling this would prove to be an entirely appropriate choice.

The music faded, and an announcer, his resonant delivery full of joyful enthusiasm, exclaimed, "Welcome to *Sexuality Unchained*, Dr. Penny's award-winning advice column of the air, covering all issues of adult sexuality!" He dropped his voice to add in a serious tone, "A warning: this is for adults only. Some material discussed may offend some listeners." Another burst of Anything Goes was followed by: "And here's Dr. Penny!"

I recalled that Harriet had said Dr. Penny began her program with a statement that sex was her great passion. Harriet wasn't wrong. "Sex is my great passion!" Pen exclaimed. "My great passion! A life not filled to the brim with healthy sensuality is no life at all! For those listeners new to *Sexuality Unchained*, let me promise you an unbridled, unrestrained, candid exploration of adult sexuality in all its wonderful diversity."

The calls began. Leaping lizards! There were some uninhibited people out there! I was no prude, but a couple of times my mouth literally fell open. Pen took it all in her stride, even the bloke who'd had a surprising experience while swimming with dolphins.

"Dolphins," said Pen approvingly. "Sexy beggars and opportunists too. You wouldn't be the only case of a cross-species romp."

"But it was male dolphin!" the bloke exclaimed in some distress. "And I'm not gay."

"Three possibilities," said Pen. "A bisexual dolphin, a homosexual dolphin, or a heterosexual dolphin with poor eyesight."

This observation generated a positive firestorm of calls, and perspiration began to run down Emily Whippet's face. Pen was obliged to state emphatically that she did not subscribe to bestiality as a way of life.

"There is no homosexuality in the animal kingdom," declared one irate woman. "These are all God's creatures, and each and every one follows God's design for natural, normal behavior."

Pen snorted at that. "Homosexual and bisexual behavior is common. In fact, it's more common in other species than in humans. Read up on bonobo chimpanzees. It'll curl your hair."

The woman snorted right back at Pen. "I doubt anything you could say would curl my hair," she sneered.

"Wrap your ears around this," said Pen with a ferocious grin. "Bonobo chimpanzees are among humankind's closest relatives. All the bonobos that have been closely observed turn out to be one hundred percent bisexual." She paused for that to sink in. "You got that? Every last chimp swings both ways."

An inarticulate cry, and the caller disconnected.

"And that, listeners, is the sound of hair curling," said Pen with satisfaction.

It was half an hour into the program that Pen's stalker called. Whippet Emily gestured from behind the glass that she had something, then, in the next commercial break, she came on through our earphones. "Creepy Guy's the call after next—calling himself 'Robert of Agoura Hills.' I'm sure it's him."

"Put him through first, as soon as the break ends." Pen looked over at me, triumphant. "I knew he'd call."

The seemingly interminable commercials finally ended. "You're listening to *Sexuality Unchained*. And we're back with Dr. Penny..."

Pen purred into the microphone, "And our next call is from Robert of Agoura Hills. What do you have for us, Robert?"

"It's what I have for you, Dr. Penny."

Although masculine, it was a high-pitched, slippery voice with an unpleasant note of insinuation.

"You have a problem with your sexuality?"

"I have a problem with you, you ball-breaking bitch."

Emily made a cutthroat gesture to indicate the ten-second delay was in operation and the caller was off the air before listeners could hear his last words.

"Do women intimidate you, Robert?" Pen inquired sweetly.

He ignored that, saying, "You'll be getting a message soon—a very lethal message. You should learn from it." He sniggered. "I wish I could see your face when it's delivered."

There was a click, and he was gone.

Disappointed, Pen sat back in her chair. "That was a bummer," she said. "He hardly said a thing."

My imagination was buzzing with possible meanings of a very lethal message. "It was a threat, Pen. The message he mentioned could be a bomb, anthrax—"

"Kylie, I've heard much worse than that from callers," said Pen with a shrug, "and nothing's ever happened."

"Five seconds," said Roger.

As cheerfully outrageous as ever, Pen continued with depressed callers suffering premature performance problems, premature rejection problems—"You must be making a lousy first impression," Pen remarked at one point—as well as upbeat callers who readily shared the most intimate particulars of their sexual experiences in surprising detail.

Near the end of the program, Pen was busily quizzing a woman who claimed to have discovered some amazing techniques while traveling in Tibet, when a movement in the control room caught my eye. I was astonished to see Rube Wasinsky, his face haggard, staring through the glass at Pen.

She saw him too. "What's wrong?" she mouthed, while the caller burbled on about secret Tibetan sex arts.

118

When he put his face in his hands, Pen turned back to the microphone. She interrupted the woman, with, "I'm so sorry, but we're out of time," then she rapidly wrapped up the show.

Pen and I took off our earphones as Rube came into the room. "Oh, Pen," he said. "Oh, Pen."

She stared at him, white-faced. "What is it?"

"It's Oscar."

Pen leaped up. "He's hurt?"

"He's dead, Pen. Oscar's dead."

SIXTEEN

Ariana arrived at UCLA before Pen, Rube, and I did. I had volunteered to drive, as Pen was so shaken and Rube was so distracted that they would have been a danger on the roads. Rube knew Oscar's body had been found near one of the university buildings presently being extensively renovated. I'd become familiar enough with the campus to make an educated guess where this might be.

As it happened, we didn't have to search for the site, as the irritating strobing of the emergency lights of several patrol cars and the white glare of spotlights made it obvious. As the death had occurred on campus, UCLA's police force was also involved. I parked quite illegally next to sign that read NO PARKING AT ANY TIME and had scarcely stopped the car before Pen was out and rushing toward the lights. Rube and I caught up with her when she slowed suddenly at the edge of the crowd that had gathered. I was sure I knew why. Pen was imagining, like I was, the horror that would be waiting for her.

Spectators, mainly students, watched everything with avid eyes. They were clustered outside the scaffolding enclosing a red-brick and sandstone four-story building. They were held back from the action by police tape, which was strung around the floodlit area.

Ariana was just inside the police tape talking with a heavily built man with a world-weary expression. Everything on his face had a downward droop—his eyelids, his cheeks, his long nose, the corners of his mouth, the flabby jowls that blurred the definition of his jaw.

Ariana gestured for us to join them. The curiosity of the crowd was aroused when we were allowed to duck under the tape. Ariana intro-

duced us to Detective Lark, a name that seemed singularly inappropri-
ate for him. As Lark made a perfunctory statement of sympathy, Pen
looked past him and shuddered.

I felt like shuddering too. It wasn't like the movies or TV—Oscar's
body hadn't been decently covered. I recalled reading somewhere that
contamination of a crime scene often occurred when bodies picked up
fibers from the material used to hide them from curious eyes. Oscar lay
facedown, his limbs splayed. Around his bushy head a dark stain—
surely blood—had seeped into the dry earth.

Pen swayed, and seized Rube's arm for support. Obviously fearing
she might collapse, Lark took her other arm and together he and Rube
helped her to the nearest patrol car.

"Pen shouldn't have seen that," I said.

"Could you have stopped her from coming here?"

I shook my head. "Of course not."

Ariana looked grim. "As next of kin, she'll be asked to identify the
body anyway."

I had the unreal feeling I was a character in a script in a TV crime
show and that any moment the director would yell, "Cut!"

I said, just as my TV character would, "What happened?"

Indicating the scaffolding looming above us, Ariana said, "It
appears Oscar fell from somewhere up there."

I could see figures on the roof silhouetted by the flashlights they
were using. "What could Oscar possibly be doing on a building site?"

Ariana shrugged. "As a cop, I found people do the strangest things,"
she said. "Without a thought of personal danger, they get themselves
into hazardous situations. Sometimes it's fatal."

My gaze was drawn magnetically to Oscar's body. If he would only
get up, and laugh, and say, "I fooled you, didn't I?" But he would never
shake that shaggy head again or exclaim, "Bloody Yarrow!"

"Ariana, are you saying this is just a stupid accident?"

"It's much too early to come to any firm conclusion, but I get the
impression Ted Lark is leaning that way."

"You know Detective Lark?"

"Very well. We worked together several times when I was on the force."

I looked over to the patrol car. Rube and Pen were in the backseat, and Detective Lark was leaning through the open door, talking to them. "Something happened tonight that maybe he should know. Pen's stalker called the program and said she'd be getting a lethal message."

My skin tingled as Ariana touched my arm. "Can you tell me exactly what he said?"

I repeated the call as best I could remember. "It's recorded, of course."

"I'll tell Ted."

As she went to walk over to the patrol car, I said, "Isn't the question to ask whose advantage it is that Oscar's dead?"

Ariana turned back to me. "You're thinking Jack Yarrow? You see the eminent professor luring Oscar to the top of this building, then shoving him over?"

"Well, yes," I said. "I can, actually."

ↄ

I didn't get upset until I was back home at Kendall & Creeling. It was almost dawn, and I felt as though I hadn't slept for days. Julia Roberts was my undoing. If only she hadn't purred the moment she saw me. I swept her up in my arms and buried my face in her fur. "Oscar Braithwaite's dead," I told her. Then the tears came.

"I don't know why I'm crying," I sniffled to Jules, who was being remarkably good about the whole thing. "It's not that I knew him well, but Oscar was my client. And he died in a horrible way."

A vivid picture of Oscar's sprawled body kept appearing in my mind. How long would it take to fall four stories? Only a second or two. Did Oscar have time to realize he was about to die, or be terribly injured? Were his last thoughts for himself, or did he think of his sister?

I'd stuck around and finally driven Pen home while Ariana drove Rube to the radio station to collect Pen's car. Pen had been beside herself with grief. It was somehow shocking to see someone usually full of bold life now so distraught. I'd stayed with her until Rube arrived, feeling totally inadequate. What could I say to comfort her? Not a thing. For want of anything else to do, I'd made her a cup of tea.

I squeezed Jules a little tighter. "Poor Pen," I said to her. "Can you even imagine how she feels?"

Jules yawned. Empathy wasn't her strong suit.

When she struggled politely, I put her down. After Jules had groomed her wet fur into a semblance of order, and I'd managed to pull myself together, and was contemplating a hot shower before I fell into bed, Ariana called.

"That was rough," she said. "Are you OK?"

Tears immediately filled my eyes. "I was until you asked me."

"Are you up to seeing her later today?"

Pen had demanded a meeting this afternoon, insisting that both Ariana and I attend. Rube had said he'd come too. We'd established we'd meet at three o'clock here at Kendall & Creeling.

"I think so." I blinked rapidly. "Sorry to be such a sook."

"Oh, Kylie, don't be so hard on yourself."

There was such warmth in her voice, I said, "Stop it!"

"What?" She sounded startled.

"Don't be so nice to me. It'll make me cry more."

A soft chuckle came down the line. "I'll try to be harsh," she said. "But it'll be difficult."

⊃

"I want you to stay on the case, Kylie." Pen Braithwaite was adamant. "Oscar would have expected it. Nail Jack Yarrow as a plagiarist..." She paused, then added, "Or worse."

As it was Sunday, and much quieter than usual in my office, all I could hear of the outside world was a distant siren and the soft rumble of traffic on Sunset Boulevard. Pen, Rube, and I sat around the coffee table I'd recently purloined from Lonnie's office, where it'd been buried under a blizzard of files and papers.

I had the errant thought of how nice it would be to do what I'd originally scheduled for myself—spend the afternoon planting

Australian-native bushes in the backyard. I'd only had time to give them a quick watering, so they'd have to survive in their pots another week.

Ariana leaned forward in her chair. "You believe Professor Yarrow had something to do with your brother's death?"

She was casually dressed in what looked like the same well-worn blue jeans she'd been wearing on Friday night. I felt a totally unseemly tug of desire.

Pen, her face gray with strain, said quietly, "I'm sure he's responsible. Yarrow's home free as far as the symposium is concerned. He'll get up in front of his peers and triumph with an address based on Oscar's findings and claim the research as his own. There'll be no one there to contradict him."

"I'll contradict him," declared Rube stoutly.

Pen patted his hand. "You're such a love to say that, but you know as well as I do that we need hard evidence." She turned to me. "Evidence that Kylie's going to obtain this coming week."

"It would help if I knew what the quokka question was," I said.

"I've no idea," said Pen. She looked at Rube. "Did Oscar confide in you?"

"Not a word."

Crikey, this was no help. "Maybe Erin Fogarty knows," I said. "She worked with Oscar in the field, so she should have a fair idea what was going on."

Pen's expression became bleak. "Erin Fogarty," she said, "broke Oscar's heart. He never got over it."

Rube was surprised. "Why, I saw them talking together on Friday. They seemed on very good terms."

"Where and when was this?" Pen demanded.

"I don't know…I think around four-thirty, when I was leaving. I was walking to my car in the parking structure when I came upon Oscar and Erin, heads together, very lovey-dovey. I didn't like to interrupt, so I pretended I hadn't seen them, got into my car, and left."

Fixing me with a hard stare, Pen said, "You're friendly with this young woman?"

"Working on it."

"Work harder. She's the key. I'm sure of it."

Ariana said, "If this is a murder case—"

"If? If!" Some of Pen's usual spirit showed in her flashing eyes. "Of course Oscar was murdered. I've held back from saying this because I know the investigation's just beginning, but I know in my heart it's true—the same way I know Yarrow had something to do with it."

"What about your stalker?" Rube said. "You know Oscar swore he was going to track him down and beat him to a pulp. And that call last night to your program was a thinly veiled threat. What if he meant the message was Oscar's death?"

I'd had this thought myself, so I waited with interest to see how Pen responded.

"It was so like Oscar to want to protect me." Her lips trembled. "And I laughed at him on Saturday morning when he said he had a lead about my stalker." A tear ran down her cheek. "I hurt his feelings. The last thing he said was that he'd show me."

I could see Pen was about to drop her bundle, so to divert her I said, "Have you opened the envelope?"

"Envelope?"

"Your brother gave us an envelope to be opened if something happened to him," said Ariana. "He said he was giving you an identical one."

"I think I shoved it in a drawer somewhere," said Pen vaguely. "I didn't take him seriously." Her face crumpled.

Rube, obviously seeing she was about to break down, stood up. Taking her arm, he said, "Come on, honey. Let's take you home."

It was an indication of Pen's misery that she didn't protest but meekly allowed herself to be led away.

I saw them out and came back to find Ariana had retrieved Oscar's creased white envelope from the safe.

"Let's have a cuppa," I said, "and we can open it then."

The kitchen was one of my favorite rooms because Ariana had first kissed me there. I couldn't help thinking about that kiss as I watched Ariana's slim fingers opening the envelope.

As I made the tea, she spread the contents out on the kitchen counter. After I'd poured us each a cup of tea—I wondered if Ariana actually liked it, or was just being polite—we examined the material Oscar had thought important enough to include in his after-death missive.

There was a photocopy of a handwritten will, leaving everything to his sister, Penelope Braithwaite. Across the top he had written "Pen has the original."

Several stapled pages were headed "Australian Megafauna." Another set of pages appeared to be an extract of research by someone named Diana Niptucker, Ph.D. The final item was a handwritten letter signed by Oscar Braithwaite.

Ariana read it aloud: "To whom it may concern. If you are reading this, then Jack Yarrow has had me killed. I won't mince words. To put it in laymen's terms, Yarrow has stolen my groundbreaking research on the relationship between contemporary quokkas and their extinct megafauna marsupial ancestors of the early Pleistocene epoch. In order to pass off my discoveries as his own, Yarrow is likely to find it necessary to eliminate the one person who can prove him a fraud, namely myself, Oscar Braithwaite, Ph.D. I repeat, if I am found dead, even in circumstances that make it seem an accident, Jack Yarrow will be responsible. Throughout his career he has stopped at nothing to inflate his reputation, no matter what the cost to others. In my case it may be my life. It is my hope, of course, that no one ever has to read this. Oscar Braithwaite."

"Detective Lark will be interested to see this letter," I said.

"It doesn't prove anything," said Ariana. "He hated Yarrow, so these accusations aren't necessarily well-founded."

"Blimey," I said, "what if Oscar committed suicide, knowing this letter had deliberately set up his great rival, Jack Yarrow?"

"You certainly have a devious mind," Ariana remarked, amused. "I was thinking, rather, that Oscar Braithwaite's death really was an accident, but this letter exists to unfairly implicate his great rival, Professor Yarrow."

"When will we have the results of the postmortem?"

"The autopsy? The week after next, if we're lucky."

"'Strewth," I said, "that long? Can't you hurry it along?"

"Do you have an idea how many autopsies are performed by the Coroner's Office in Los Angeles every week?"

"A lot?"

"And then some."

I gathered up the stapled sheets. "You take the letter for Detective Lark. I'll read through this other stuff and see if I can make any sense of it."

Ariana stood up, stretched, then covered a yawn with her hand. "We both need an early night," she said.

I just looked at her.

I never seen her blush before. "No, Kylie," she said. "No."

"Why not?"

She didn't meet my eyes. "We have to talk but not now."

"I'm not going to play detective," I said. "I'll wait for you to tell me what it is that makes it so impossible for us to—"

Actions speak louder than words, my mum always said. I took Ariana in my arms and kissed her. For a moment she responded, then she pushed me away. "This isn't going to work."

I didn't say anything as she prepared to leave. At the front door she paused. "The last thing I want to do is hurt you."

"Then don't."

She shook her head. "You make it sound so easy. And it isn't."

I stood there for a long time after she had gently closed the door behind her.

SEVENTEEN

I was exhausted, but that night I couldn't get to sleep. Thoughts rocketed around in my skull like maddened billiard balls until I despaired of ever getting any rest. Eventually, I gave up trying and, leaving Julia Roberts curled up at the end of the bed, went to make myself a glass of warm milk.

My mum always maintained warm milk beat any sleeping pill hollow, but it didn't work for me. Not feeling even faintly sleepy, I padded into my office and turned on my computer.

I had scanned through the papers from Oscar's envelope before I went to bed, and had some vague idea of what the quokka question might be. The pages headed "Australian Megafauna" were written in dense scientific language, but I got the general drift. Up until the Pleistocene epoch, only 20,000 years ago, Australia had been populated by an extraordinary number of gigantic species, many of which were jumbo versions of present-day marsupials. *Diprotodon optatum* was an enormous marsupial wombat the size of a rhinoceros, *Procoptodon goliah* a colossal kangaroo. There was even a huge carnivorous marsupial lion, *Thylacoleo carnifex*. Then, in the late Ice Age, these animals became extinct, the only evidence of their presence the fossils that they had left and the legends of the Aborigines.

The other scientific item in the envelope had been an extract of research by Diana Niptucker, Ph.D. The language had been so full of scientific jargon I'd given up it. Now, since I was awake anyway, I decided to use my time profitably and Google "Dr. Diana Niptucker." I reckoned she had an unusual name, so I wouldn't have to wade through a zillion possibilities to find out who she was.

Diana Niptucker turned out to be an expert on the fossils of the megafauna period. I got the impression she was regarded by the scientific community with some reserve, as she espoused rather radical theories about the extinction of Australia's huge marsupials. I was pleased to find she had a Web site, and that on that site she provided an e-mail address.

I whipped off an e-mail to her explaining that Dr. Oscar Braithwaite had hired Kendall & Creeling to investigate a contentious matter between himself and Professor Jack Yarrow. Dr. Braithwaite had referred to the quokka question but had not explained exactly what this was. As Dr. Braithwaite had recently met with an unfortunate accident—I thought it was wiser not to mention murder as a possibility—I wondered whether she, Dr. Niptucker, could throw any light on the matter of the quokka question.

Feeling I'd accomplished something, I sat back to consider whether it was worthwhile going back to bed. Probably not, as I still didn't feel sleepy. I looked at the Google logo on the screen. I could type in Natalie Ives's name and see what came up. I'd told Ariana I wouldn't play detective, but what would be the harm?

It took me ten seconds to decide I couldn't do it. Ariana would tell me in her own time. But what would she tell me? That she was committed to someone else? My mind skittered around the possibilities I'd considered a thousand times: Ariana was in love with a married woman who wouldn't leave her husband and kids; Ariana was totally devoted to the memory of someone who had died; Ariana pined for someone unattainable, who was in jail, or in the witness protection scheme, or on some covert mission overseas.

This was getting me nowhere. My glance fell on the undisturbed pile of garden shed brochures. Might as well look at them now. I spent the next few minutes reading through optimistic words about the wisdom of purchasing each particular brand of shed. I yawned. Maybe the warm milk was working after all.

Ↄ

I slept but not well. About dawn, when I was thinking I might as well get up, I fell into an exhausted slumber so heavy I didn't wake until I opened bleary eyes, hearing the unmistakable sounds of activity in the nearby kitchen, followed by an angry exchange. I couldn't make out the words, but the voices were those of Fran and Melodie.

I showered in haste, flung on casual student clothes—jeans, sneakers, and a T-shirt—and set off to get a fast bowl of porridge before I left for UCLA and another day of hard work preparing for the Global Marsupial Symposium.

I entered the kitchen to find Melodie and Lonnie but no Fran. Her expression thunderous, Melodie was toying with a bagel and cream cheese. Lonnie was chomping his way through a McDonald's pancake breakfast.

"Health food again?" I remarked to him.

"Our Melodie's upset," said Lonnie in a stage whisper. "Speak kindly to her."

"What's the matter?"

"Treachery," said Melodie, with a brisk hair toss. "That's what's the matter. I've been stabbed in the back."

Lonnie grinned at me. "Things didn't go terribly well at the auditions for Quip's play."

"Ashlee?" I said to Melodie. "She's been cast as Lucy/Lucas?"

"Not Ashlee," said Melodie with icy disdain. "Fran."

I was gobsmacked. "Fran's been cast as Lucy/Lucas?"

"How do you spell preferential treatment?" Melodie demanded.

I rightly assumed this was a rhetorical question, but Lonnie, grinning, obediently began to spell the words, and only stopped when Melodie slapped the side of his head.

"Ow! That hurt."

"Good," she snapped.

"I never realized Fran had ambitions to be an actor," I remarked.

Lonnie, nursing his ear, hooted. "Sweetheart, half of L.A. is writing a screenplay. The other half has ambitions to be an actor. It's that kind of town."

"The betrayal," announced Melodie, "is what hurts. Larry-my-agent says I have to roll with the punches, but as I said to Larry, it pierces your heart when a friend is disloyal."

"Disloyal?" Fran said from the doorway. "Oh, please! All I did was audition for a part."

"All you did," said Melodie in a cutting tone, "was to totally ruin the chances of someone with real acting ability to play a part she was born to play."

"Real acting ability?" said Fran with an acid smile on her china-doll face. "And who would that be?"

"Whoops," said Lonnie, "I'm outta here." He winked at me. "Battle of the Titans. And you've got a front-row seat."

"If Quip wasn't your husband, no way would you have a chance of getting that part." Melodie was all icy scorn. "Like, you've never even taken an acting class."

"You leave Quip out of this!"

"Besides," said Melodie with a sneer. "You're so short. No stage presence at all."

Crikey, Fran in full rage mode was a disturbing sight. "Short, am I?" she snarled, bouncing on her toes.

"Tiny, insignificant," snapped Melodie back at her.

"That's enough," I said. They both looked at me. I went on, as cool as Ariana, "Argue in your own time, not Kendall & Creeling's."

I held my breath. Calling their bluff was a dangerous strategy. If it didn't work, it would leave me looking weak.

Melodie was the first to speak. "This is all your fault, Fran," she said with dignity, before sweeping out of the room, her chin in the air.

Not letting my relief show, I said to Fran, "I've looked at the stuff you gave me on garden sheds. I can't see any are really suitable. We need something better, more substantial. There must be companies who'll supply and erect prefabricated structures that will better meet our needs."

"It'll cost more," said Fran.

"That's OK as long as we end up with something we can use."

We spent the next few minutes discussing the specifications, then Fran went off looking pleased, having been given the go-ahead to negotiate a deal on behalf of our company.

Ariana's coffee mug was missing, so I used my detecting skills to deduce she was probably in her office. She was, looking svelte in black. I described how I'd found Diana Niptucker's Web site last night, and sent her an e-mail requesting any information she had. Then I told Ariana I'd given Fran authority to purchase a storage structure, pending our final approval.

Ariana raised an eyebrow. "Tell me again why we need this extra space. Is it just because of Fran's disaster supplies?"

"Well, that's part of it, of course, but I did have an idea for some minor alterations."

"Why am I not surprised?"

I grinned at her sardonic tone, then told her my plan for taking over the present storage area for my sitting room, getting a bit carried away and waving my hands around. I finished with, "It'll be terrif to have more space."

"So you're here for the long haul?"

I frowned. "You mean am I staying? You know I'm not going home to Oz."

"You haven't thought of moving into something larger?"

"This suits me and Jules."

"Well," said Ariana, "we'd better work on finding somewhere to store the disaster supplies."

"I'm on it full bore," I said. "To the max."

Ariana cast a proprietary look around her black-and-white office. "But my room is off-limits, OK?"

"'Strewth," I said, "that's put a spoke in my wheel. I was planning to knock down a wall or two here."

Ariana laughed, then sobered. "You are joking, right?"

"I may be," I said over my shoulder as I skipped out the door.

Driving along Sunset Boulevard to the campus, I had a sudden, jolting thought. I shook my head to unscramble my brains. When Ariana had mentioned me moving to something larger, she couldn't have met moving in with her, could she?

It was a lovely idea, and it buoyed me through two sets of red traffic lights and three SUV drivers rudely cutting in front of me. Then reality came crashing down. Ariana didn't want my love, so why would she desire my company? What she'd really been hinting at was that I should get out of Kendall & Creeling's building and into an apartment.

I arrived at the biology department in a bleak mood—not the state of mind required for my main task today, which was to win Erin Fogarty's friendship. Still, dissembling was a private eye's stock in trade, so I plastered a pleasant expression over my inner angst and headed for Georgia Tapp's office.

On Friday everyone had received a memo advising that in the last days before the symposium, Georgia Tapp would be coordinating all administrative matters. From now on, first thing every morning, all staff concerned with the event were to report to her office for instructions. Because I'd slept in and stopped to talk with Ariana, I was running late, so I got my apologies ready.

Outside Georgia's office I ran into Zoran Pestle, who headed the committee set up by Yarrow to handle the organizational details of the symposium. He was the dark, intense sort at the best of times, but today he looked positively sinister. Gesturing toward Georgia's door, he hissed, "She's a fat spider sitting in the middle of her sticky web, pulling strings and railroading everyone who gets in her way."

For a moment I admired Zoran's mastery of mixed metaphor. "Georgia, you mean?"

His dark eyes narrowed until I wondered if he could see more than a narrow strip of light. "Yes, Georgia Tapp," he spat out. "What is she but a mere administrative assistant? I ask you, does she have a higher degree? Any degree? Has she the right, the knowledge, the experience to tell someone like me what to do?"

"Must be upsetting."

Zoran peered at me suspiciously. "You're only a graduate student," he said, "so you can't possibly appreciate the mores of the upper stratum of academia."

"Too true," I said.

As I spoke, Georgia's head popped out of her office door, giving us both quite a start. "What are you wasting time standing out there for?" she demanded. "Professor Yarrow has called an urgent meeting to discuss the tragic events of Saturday evening. You should be there now at this moment."

Zoran nodded. Obviously, he knew about Oscar Braithwaite's death. I hadn't had time to read the paper this morning, but guessed there would have been an item about a visiting academic's body being found on UCLA grounds.

As Zoran and I scooted off to join the meeting, he gave me the benefit of his advice. "Georgia can seem very sweet, but she's pure poison. You're inexperienced. You could be fooled."

"I'll do my best not to cross to the dark side," I said cheerfully.

Zoran shot me a puzzled look, as though he found it almost impossible to believe that I might be treating a warning from a man with a higher degree so lightly.

"We're here," I said, pushing the metal bar that opened one side of the lecture hall double-door. The room had raked seating, and we'd come in at the top row, so I reckoned we had a good chance of sneaking in unnoticed.

No such luck. Yarrow, standing at the front with a microphone stand, stopped in mid sentence to say sarcastically, "So nice of you to make it."

"G'day, Prof."

Someone laughed. Yarrow was not amused. His thin-lipped mouth turned sour, and his prominent eyes bulged a little more.

He cleared his throat. "As I was saying before I was so rudely interrupted, Dr. Oscar Braithwaite's tragic demise must not be allowed to impact upon the Global Marsupial Symposium. Yes, it's true he was to deliver a keynote address, but I, myself, will step into the breech with my own original contribution to the quokka debate."

While he'd been talking, I'd been checking out the audience, looking for the future target of my charm, Erin Fogarty. I expected to find her in the front row, gazing adoringly at her hero, but finally spotted her skinny figure at the end of the second back row. It would be simple to manage things so I'd meet up with her as we were leaving the lecture hall.

"What about Penny Braithwaite?" a woman called out. "Are we sending condolences?"

"Of course," Yarrow said. "Dr. Penelope Braithwaite is a colleague—a rather notorious one, I'm afraid, but still a colleague. Arrangements will be made to send flowers and a suitable card expressing our commiserations."

"Deep commiserations," someone offered.

Yarrow scowled. "Oh, very well. Deep commiserations."

"How about deep, sincere commiserations?"

"That's quite enough discussion on the wording of our card of sympathy," said Yarrow firmly. He brushed his hands together in a we've-finished-with-this-topic manner. "And now—"

"How did Dr. Braithwaite die?" a grizzled old bloke called out. "The few lines in the paper this morning said he'd been found dead on Saturday night. No details."

Yarrow ran a hand over his high, domed forehead. "A fall, I believe."

Someone else said loudly, "I heard Dr. Braithwaite tumbled off scaffolding in a construction site on campus. Some of my students told me about it this morning."

A buzz of speculation filled the room. "What was he doing in a construction site in the first place?" someone asked.

Yarrow tapped his microphone, causing an irritating bop-bop noise, until the hum of voices died away. "If I may make a comment, I've had occasion, over the years, to spend a little time with Dr. Braithwaite. I don't believe I insult his memory to say he was not a cautious man, but he was a deeply curious one. I imagine he decided to explore the building undergoing renovation, and simply lost his balance, and sadly, fell. I gather he didn't suffer. His extensive head injuries made his death virtually instantaneous."

"But what was he doing in a building site at night?"

"I've no idea." Clearly, Jack Yarrow considered he'd spent enough time on the topic. "Now, on to more pressing matters. It's vital our Global Marsupial Symposium be a resounding success. I hope I can rely on each and every one of you to pull your weight and make sure it is. And one last thing, if you haven't already checked your daily work schedule with Ms. Tapp, please go to her office immediately and collect the information."

I joined the stream of people exiting at the top entry doors, timing it so I'd end up next to Erin Fogarty. "Erin," I said, megafriendly, "bonzer to see you."

"Hello."

"I'm Kylie, remember?"

She nodded absently. This sheila looked like the weight of the world was on her narrow shoulders. Her face was all blotchy, and her nose was pink. Maybe, when Rube Wasinsky had seen Oscar and Erin together on Friday, they'd been getting together again, after the breakup in Western Australia, and now she was heartbroken at his death.

"Awful about Dr. Braithwaite," I said.

She hung her head. "Yes, awful." A few tears dripped down her front.

"There, there," I said, putting a sympathetic arm around her.

Erin lifted her head and looked at me directly. "I killed him," she said. "It's my fault."

EIGHTEEN

The detecting gods smiled on me, for when I got my assignment for the day from Georgia Tapp, I was rostered with Erin Fogarty, our task being to collate the individual information packets that were to be given out to each attendee at the first day registration.

After Erin's revelation as we'd left the lecture hall, she'd had a bit of a crying jag, and I hadn't been able to get another coherent word from her. She'd tottered into the nearest ladies' room to wash her face, and I'd headed for Georgia's office.

Actually, there was another surprise there for me. I'd knocked politely on the door, and been told to enter. Georgia wasn't alone.

"Sorry," I said, "didn't mean to interrupt."

I'd never met the hulking man standing beside Georgia's desk, but I immediately recognized his too-small shaved head, his beady eyes, and his grossly overdeveloped body. In his photos Wally Easton, Yarrow's ex-brother-in-law, had looked unappealing—in person he was downright menacing.

"Come in, dear," said Georgia, all sweetness and light.

"G'day," I said to Wally Easton.

Easton's flat stare passed over me without interest. He didn't bother replying. I noticed he had disproportionately small, lobeless ears set flat to his skull. Somewhere I'd read that ears like that indicated antisocial tendencies.

"What are you looking at?" he asked belligerently.

He had a high, reedy voice. With a pulse of excitement I realized it was a good fit with Pen's caller on Saturday night.

Both Georgia and Easton were looking at me, waiting for my reply. It didn't seem safe to comment on his criminal ears, so I said, "I was just wondering if you shaved your skull, or if you used one of those hair-removing creams."

"Is she for real?" he demanded of Georgia, who looked embarrassed on my behalf.

"Australian," she said to him, as if that explained everything.

He grunted. Georgia handed me my assignment, and I skedaddled.

I found Erin Fogarty in the lecture room temporarily assigned for symposium matters. She was listlessly sliding items into envelopes and checking off names against a list.

"Are you feeling better?" I asked. Her eyes immediately filled with tears. Apparently not.

We were alone, at least for the moment, so I went directly to the matter at hand. "How could you blame yourself for Dr. Braithwaite's death? It was an accident, wasn't it?"

She looked at me with tragic, red-rimmed eyes. "I hope so."

"You hope so?"

Erin sniffed loudly. "If it wasn't for me, he wouldn't have been there. I'm sure that's true."

I tried a puzzled expression—not hard because I was. "I'm not sure what you mean."

"Oscar—Dr. Braithwaite—believed he was meeting me."

"You made a date to meet Oscar on the building site?"

Erin's weak chin trembled. "I did it for Professor Yarrow. How was I to know someone would get hurt?"

"Let's get this straight," I said. "Jack Yarrow asked you to set up a rendezvous with Oscar Braithwaite on top of the building he later fell off?"

Erin drooped her long neck, rather like a dispirited swan. "Not exactly."

Reining in an impulse to shake her until her teeth rattled, I said in a kindly, confiding tone, "Tell me all about it, Erin. You'll feel so much better when you do. My mum always says that a problem shared is a problem halved."

"What do you think of Georgia?"

"Georgia?" Crikey, I was sounding like an echo. "I hardly know her, but she seems nice."

'Nice,' I thought, was a safe word, which combined with 'seems,' didn't commit me to a definite view, so I could shift to agree with Erin, if necessary.

"Seems nice," said Erin. "Seems."

"This has something to do with Dr. Braithwaite falling off the roof?"

"Georgia took me aside and said she had a confidential task for me to do. She told me Jack—Professor Yarrow, that is—wanted me to meet with Oscar and tell him I'd realized I was wrong about Professor Yarrow and that he did steal Oscar's work." She sent me a fierce look, her cheeks glowing in pink indignation. "It isn't true. Dr. Yarrow was taking back what was his in the first place."

I clasped my hands and put an honest but naïve expression on my face. "No! You're telling me Dr. Braithwaite stole research from Professor Yarrow? Why wasn't he denounced?"

"Denounced?"

Obviously Erin was developing my echo problem. "Why wasn't Oscar accused," I said. "Condemned, publicly humiliated, forced to admit his heinous academic sins?"

When she blinked at me uncomprehendingly, I spelled it out. "If Professor Yarrow believed his research material had been stolen by Dr. Braithwaite, why didn't he take steps to have this academic theft exposed? Why steal it back in an underhanded way?"

She looked relieved. "Oh, I see what you mean. It's simple, really. It was very sensitive material, a new discovery that would turn quokka research on its ear. Professor Yarrow didn't want to provoke a scandal because the information would get out prematurely."

"I'm a bit lost," I said. "What has Georgia got to do with all this?"

"I think she's in love with him," said Erin, plainly bitter.

The sheila was getting me het-up, the way she was jumping all over the place. I calmed myself by mentally referring to *Private Investigation: The Complete Handbook*. There was a chapter on interrogation techniques. I recalled one piece of advice: Be a friend. Make the witness want to tell you everything.

"Erin," I said, "you've been through a lot. People have expected so much of you, but they haven't treated you with the respect you deserve."

She sat up straighter. "You're right, you know, Carol. I wouldn't have said it myself, but yes, it's true."

"Kylie," I said. "The name's Kylie, not Carol."

She blushed, which together with her pink eyes and nose made her look positively rosy. "Oh, sorry. I'm just so upset I don't know what I'm saying."

To get her back on track, I said, "About Georgia—Zoran Pestle doesn't get on too well with her. He told me he thinks of her as a 'fat spider in a web.'"

Erin nodded vigorously. "He could be right." She clutched my hand, at the same time looking around the room for eavesdroppers. "I really believed Georgia was telling me what Professor Yarrow wanted me to do," she whispered, "but when I asked him face-to-face, he said he didn't know what I was talking about."

I was fed up with going around in circles. "Erin," I said firmly, "spit it out. What exactly did Georgia tell you to do?"

"I thought it was what he wanted," she wailed.

"Keep calm," I said, more to myself than Erin Fogarty.

She sniffed, swallowed, and thus fortified, began with, "Georgia asked me to get a message to Oscar that I wanted to meet him on Friday afternoon in the parking structure everyone in the department uses. I was to tell him that I…" She trailed off, blushing yet again.

"Yes?" I said encouragingly.

"I was to tell Oscar I still loved him and that I could get the evidence he needed to prove Professor Yarrow had stolen his research. I said I'd send a text message to his cell phone to say where and when we'd meet in the weekend." She snuffled and wiped her eyes. "Georgia told me to say we'd meet somewhere on campus, but it would have to be where no one would see me because I was afraid of Dr. Yarrow."

At last we'd got somewhere. For clarification, I said, "So you text-messaged Oscar to meet you at the building site on Saturday night?"

"Nooooo!"

I was startled. So was a meek-looking bloke on the point of entering the room, who gave Erin a horrified look and shot off.

"No? You didn't tell him that?"

"Georgia told me she'd handle that side of things. All I had to do was say I'd get a message to him." A sob racked her skinny body. "And I sent him to his death!"

I patted her shoulder. Surely she'd cry herself dry sometime soon. "This can all be sorted out," I said reassuringly. "You tell the police what Georgia told you to do, and they'll take it from there."

A few more body-wracking sobs greeted my observation. When she could talk, Erin cried, "You don't understand! When I saw Georgia this morning and asked her why, pretending to be me, she'd sent Oscar to that building site, do you know what she said?"

"Search me."

"Georgia said she didn't know what I was talking about—that we'd never had the conversation on Friday, that I was delusional and needed professional help urgently!"

"'Strewth," I said, "you've been set up."

"You believe me? Jack didn't." She added quickly, "But he was very kind. He said I'd been working too hard, and had got confused."

"So Jack Yarrow said he knew nothing about this plan that he himself was supposed to have hatched."

"It's not his fault," said Erin, loyal to the last. "Georgia was lying when she said Jack was involved. He knew nothing about it, I'm sure. He's not that kind of man. Why, he—"

She broke off as Winona Worsack glided into the room wearing her usual long medieval dress, her dark hair loose on her shoulders. "You!" she exclaimed, pointing a long, imperious forefinger at Erin. "How dare you besmirch the name of Jack Yarrow! How dare you!"

"But, I—"

"Don't speak. I know what's been going on. You imagine yourself in love with my husband. Deluded wretch. Poor, sick creature. You are to stop pestering him immediately."

"He pestered me first!" shouted Erin, showing some spirit at last.

141

"That's why I fell in love with him."

"That's quite enough, you stupid little ninny."

I was admiring Winona's vocabulary, having never heard anyone use 'besmirch' in conversation before, and 'ninny' only rarely, when she turned her attention in my direction. Crooking her finger, she commanded, "Kylie Kendall, come with me."

"Are you all right?" I said to Erin, not wanting to leave her distressed.

Anger had stiffened her spine. "I'll cope," she said. She shot Winona Worsack a mutinous look. "You don't understand him. You never have. Jack told me so."

Winona snorted. I felt like snorting, myself. Could Jack Yarrow actually trotted out that ancient cliché and said his wife didn't understand him?

Winona, of course, had to have the last word. "Idiot," she said and swept out of the room before Erin could respond.

"See you later," I said to Erin as I hastened to the door. I didn't want Winona to give me the slip.

"Jack can't leave her," Erin said. "He told me she swore she'll kill herself if he does. That's why he stays with her."

Blimey! This sheila had turned naïve into an art form.

⊃

"And then," I said to Ariana, "I galloped down the hall after Winona Worsack, who gets a fair speed up on the wheels she seems to have instead of feet, since she glides so smoothly."

It was early evening. We were in Ariana's office, everyone else had gone home, and I was giving her a rundown of my day.

Ariana laughed. "A beguiling picture. What happened next?"

"Winona takes me to Yarrow's office. There he is with Georgia Tapp, both long-faced. 'We have a problem,' he says to me, 'and you appear to be friendly with Erin Fogarty, so you can be of assistance, I believe.'

"And I say, 'Anything I can do to help.' Yarrow looks at Georgia, and she says on cue, 'Erin came to me this morning with the most outlandish story. She accused me of being involved in Dr. Oscar Braithwaite's death. Even more outrageous, she also claimed that Professor Yarrow was the mastermind behind the scheme. I can only think the poor girl is unbalanced.'

"At this point, there's a fair bit of grave head-shaking all round, then Yarrow asks, 'Did Erin say anything to you while you were with her this morning?'

" 'Well, yes, she did,' I say, and I outline the major points of the story, a lot more straightforwardly than Erin managed to give it to me.

"Everyone looks grim. Jack Yarrow says, superindignant, 'I can't imagine why she wants to attack me.' His wife sends a nasty smile his way. 'Because you seduced the silly little fool, Jack. And now you're trying to get out from under. I can understand her motivation—she wants revenge.' "

"Nice and direct," said Ariana, "but is it true?"

"Erin never mentioned being given the heave-ho by Yarrow, but she's not the most worldly graduate student on the block, so it's on the cards she hasn't noticed yet."

Ariana looked thoughtful. "Why do you think they bought you in?"

"To back up their theory that Erin's lost it. She sobbed most of the time I was with her, and it was hard work getting a coherent story out of her, but I didn't think for one moment she was bonkers."

"Consider this," said Ariana. "Maybe Erin is stringing you along. She set up the rendezvous with Oscar and was there when he fell, either by accident or because she pushed him. Now she comes up with this conspiracy narrative, killing two birds with one stone. She punishes Yarrow for ending their affair, and she implicates a rival, namely Georgia Tapp."

"Could be," I said, "but the tears she shed were real. She couldn't act that well."

"They could be genuine tears because she's lost the man she's hopelessly in love with."

I loved doing this brainstorming with Ariana. I beamed at her across the desk. "But if Erin is telling the absolute truth, we then have two possibilities. The first, that Georgia's cooked this up all on her own, and is lying through her teeth when she says Jack Yarrow instigated it. The second is that Yarrow came up with the plan and co-opted Georgia to help him out so that there'd be no direct link between him and Oscar's death."

"Where does Winona Worsack fit in?" Ariana inquired.

"She's worried about Jack Yarrow's rep, I reckon. Otherwise, I can't see why she'd care one way or the other about what Oscar might do at the symposium."

"You've studied the science of detecting liars," said Ariana. "So who's lying and who's telling the truth?"

"You're having a dig at me," I said.

My *Complete Handbook* contained several chapters on lying, and I'd made a goal to master lie detection techniques. My mistake had been to let anyone know what I was doing. Fran, in particular, had made life hard for a few days.

Ariana laughed. "Only a gentle dig. And I really want to know what you think."

"Right-oh. Erin is pretty well telling the truth, although, of course, she has no idea how much of what she's been told is accurate. Georgia? She's crooked as a dog's hind leg, but some of what she said must be true. The problem is, which bit? And I don't like Jack Yarrow, so I'm biased. It's possible he isn't involved. There's only Georgia's word that he is, and now she denies she even said it to Erin."

Picking up the phone, Ariana said, "I'm going to run this past Ted Lark. He'll certainly want to interview Erin Fogarty. And I'll mention you saw Wally Easton, and think he might be a possibility for Pen's stalker. I'd say, however, at least for the moment, Ted will want to concentrate on Erin Fogarty."

I thought with a pang how upset she'd been that morning. "Erin's pretty upset at the moment. She won't take tough questioning well."

"I'll tell him to be kind," said Ariana.

I left her dialing, and went into the kitchen to feed Julia Roberts. About time, her expression said. "Salmon tonight, Jules. Gourmet stuff."

Watching her eat—she was not a particularly refined as a diner—I began to brood. I was having myself on, thinking I could learn to be a P.I. Hey, I couldn't even tell who was lying to me. I wasn't a private detective's bootlace.

I forced myself to be honest. It was Ariana gently mocking me that had started this downward trend in my mood. It was Ariana having a secret she wouldn't tell me. It was me loving Ariana and her not loving me…

"I'm going to have it out with her," I said to Jules. "Right now."

Jules kept on eating.

NINETEEN

She looked up when I opened her office door. Without ceremony, I said, "Do you still want to buy my fifty-one percent of Kendall & Creeling?"

Clearly surprised, Ariana said, "You've changed your mind? It's for sale?"

"Not really. I was wondering if you even now had hopes of buying me out."

Ariana sat back in her chair, her expression unreadable. She knew from experience I was unlikely to let a silence stretch very long without breaking it. This time would be different, I told myself.

I felt a flicker of sour triumph when she spoke first. "I haven't mentioned the subject lately, so why are you bringing it up now?"

I hadn't meant to say them, but the words tumbled out. "If you bought me out, Ariana, you'd get rid of me. I'd get out of your life."

"Kylie, do you really think that's what I want?"

"I don't know what you want. That's the problem."

We both knew I wasn't referring to our jointly-owned company. We sat there, one on either side of her black desk, staring at each other. Ariana looked away first.

"All right," she said, "I'll tell you what you need to know, but not here. Let's go up to my place. We can sit down, enjoy a drink"—she gave a small, sardonic laugh—"and have a civilized conversation."

She went in her car: I went in mine. It was getting dark, and the curving road up into the Hollywood Hills seemed subtly ominous. It was leading to…what? I was cold with apprehension. Whatever she would tell me would make a difference; of that I was sure. The quality of that difference was the unknown factor.

Gussie greeted us with enthusiasm. German shepherds are such handsome, personable dogs. "You have presence, Gussie," I said to her. "It's an admirable characteristic." She smiled, obviously agreeing with me.

Ariana poured two glasses of red wine and gave me one. I took it to be polite. I didn't want anything to drink.

We sat opposite each other in her rose-colored lounge chairs, a low table between us. Beside us was a long plate glass window that provided a stunning view of Los Angeles at night, stretched out in patterns of light.

"Kylie, this is so hard. I'm not sure how to begin." She looked out a the city lights, so far below us. "What do you think I'm going to say?"

"I reckon you're going to tell me there's someone else."

Ariana gazed at me for a long, long moment. Then she said, "There is someone else."

I believed I'd prepared myself to hear something like this, but it was still a sickening jolt. "Who is it?"

"Does it matter?"

A pulse of anger sharpened my voice. "Of course it matters, Ariana. It matters a lot." When she didn't respond, I said, "She gave you that ring, didn't she?"

Ariana looked down at the heavy gold signet ring she always wore. "Yes."

"It's Natalie Ives, isn't it?"

Such raw pain filled her face that I was stunned. "Oh, Ariana," I said, "I'm so sorry…"

She let out her breath in a long sigh. "I'll tell you everything, Kylie. And then you'll…you'll understand how impossible it is for us—" She broke off and shook her head. "I haven't been fair to you."

"Be fair to me now. Let me in on the secret."

"Secret?" Her lips twisted. "Some secret."

My heart was thudding, not with passion but with fear. "Go on. Please."

Ariana took a sip of her drink, put it down, and after a deep breath, began. "I met Natalie when I was a rookie cop in the LAPD and she was an eminent English professor at UCLA. I was in my early twenties, Natalie was forty-one. I was dazzled by her wit, her knowledge, the sheer excitement of being with her. For my part, I adored her from the beginning but was amazed when Natalie fell in love with me."

She paused, looked at me for the first time since she'd mentioned Natalie's name. "Natalie wasn't in the closet, but I was. The macho atmosphere of the LAPD at the time was so hostile to gays that being out wasn't a realistic option. For simple self-preservation I kept our relationship secret at work. Your father was one of my closest friends. He too was concealing the fact he was gay."

I thought with a stab of grief how I'd never really known my father. Ariana had been closer to him than I'd ever been.

Ariana, her shoulders resolutely squared, continued in her clear, cool voice. "Natalie loved the water, so we pooled our resources-mine weren't great at that stage-and bought a little house near the beach in Santa Monica." A reminiscent smile lit her face. "We had so much fun renovating that little place. We painted walls; we raided yard sales; we planted a garden, even acquired a kitten."

"Priscilla?"

"Yes, Priscilla."

For a moment, Ariana seemed lost in memories. I said, "And then what happened?"

"Nothing happened, at least not for a long time. We were so happy together. Every day with Natalie was a delight. Career-wise, I advanced in the LAPD, and Natalie gained even more renown in academic circles. Our life was close to perfect. Then one day, Natalie was unexpectedly late. When she finally arrived she was confused and upset. She told me she'd got lost, driving home from UCLA, although she'd driven from Westwood to Santa Monica countless times and knew every route, every back street, every shortcut."

Ariana drew an uneven breath. "I can still remember how a chill of dread touched me, even as I reassured Natalie that this had happened because she was overworked and tired. Suddenly, little incidents over the past year I'd not remarked upon—things Natalie had forgotten to do, the times she mixed up people's names, the faint puzzled expression she sometimes wore—became terribly significant."

Ariana's expression was achingly sad. "A few days later I found Natalie crying brokenheartedly. She said that something was terribly wrong, that more and more a gray heaviness was clouding her mind." Ariana's eyes filled with tears. "Her fine, elegant mind."

I wanted to go over to her, to comfort her, but knew I couldn't. Instead, I said, "Alzheimer's disease?"

She nodded slowly. "The diagnosis was early-onset Alzheimer's. We told each other it'd be OK, but both of us knew we were lying. Natalie and I did the round of specialists. We tried every treatment they suggested, but it was clear the disease was inexorably advancing. Natalie was distraught when she realized what lay ahead for both of us. I remember her saying that she felt she was slowly dissolving, becoming less of herself every day."

I said nothing. What could I say? I tried to visualize what it must have been like for Ariana—for both of them—but I knew the reality had to be much worse than I could imagine.

Ariana got up and moved restlessly about the room. "Natalie couldn't bear for anyone to know what was happening to her. I promised her I'd keep it secret from everyone but a few close friends. She took early retirement and dropped out of academic circles altogether. I tried to arrange my workload to spend every possible moment with her. Soon it became obvious that being a cop and looking after Natalie were not compatible. I had irregular hours, was expected to be available on short notice, often at night. Natalie was becoming more dependent and needed a structured, fixed routine to help her cope."

"That's where my dad comes in?"

Ariana sat down opposite me again. "Your dad was wonderful. Colin and Ken, his partner, had often made up a foursome with Natalie and me. When she was diagnosed with Alzheimer's, they were both so supportive. A few years earlier, your father had left the LAPD and started Kendall Investigative Services. He offered me a partnership, pointing out that I could schedule my time so Natalie would have that necessary routine in her life. It was a wrench to leave the force, but I'd do anything for her, and for a long time it worked out well. I employed a retired nurse to be her companion during the day, and I was there for Natalie every night."

Ariana fixed me with her blue, intense gaze. "I promised her I would always love her, always be there for her—would never leave her." She looked down at her hands. "I underestimated Alzheimer's and overestimated myself."

Where was Natalie now? Was she in some care facility? Or had she died? If it were me, I thought I'd rather cease to exist than face such inescapable deterioration of my mind, and eventually, my body.

"I kept her at home with me as long as I could. But it became impossible. It was obvious Natalie needed twenty-four hour professional care. It was the hardest thing I ever did, to put her away in an intensive-care home."

Her lips trembled. I wished with all my heart I could simply take her in my arms and say everything will be all right. But of course, it wouldn't.

After a moment Ariana continued, "She went without fuss or tears-I was the one who wept. I go to see her at least once every week. Outwardly she's the woman I've loved for so many years, but inwardly there are only flickers of her true self. She only sometimes recognizes me. Often I can see she's puzzled but polite to this stranger who seems to know her so well."

She gave me her direct, cool look. "Now you know."

"Now I know."

"And you see why it's impossible for us-you and me."

A wave of protest rose in my throat. "I don't see why it's impossible at all."

Ariana's face hardened. "I made Natalie two promises: to always love her, and to never leave her. I broke the second promise. The first I'll never break."

TWENTY

Tuesday morning I felt groggy from lack of sleep. Horribly aware that I'd been venturing into an emotional minefield, I'd left Ariana shortly after she had responded so negatively to my protest that a relationship between us was not, as she claimed, impossible. When I'd finally forced myself to go to bed, the whole scene kept replaying over and over in my head. And when I dozed, I dreamed disjointed, disturbing dreams, full of loss and grief.

To finish off a perfect evening, Mum had called me just before I turned out the light.

"Am I disturbing something, darling?"

"No, Mum, of course not."

"Are you sure?"

Sorry for myself, I wanted to snap, *Yes, Mum, you're disturbing something—the day I found out I'm doomed to pine forever for a woman I adore so much it hurts.* I said, "I'm sure."

"I got your letter today." Her tone was gloomy. "Your handwriting indicates you're not being entirely honest with me, Kylie."

I was short with her. "I don't see how it can, since I was."

"You may not realize you're not telling the whole truth," my mum conceded, "but handwriting never lies."

I didn't say anything but silently cursed the day my mother had decided to do that handwriting analysis course at Wollegudgerie High.

Mum cleared her throat, which usually signaled she was about to embark on a new subject. "I don't know if you realize how very disturbing it is for a mother to have her only child living in a dangerous

151

place like Los Angeles."

Oh, groan!

To counterattack, I said, "Why didn't you tell me I was on an Australian TV show? I had to hear about it from someone else."

"Who?" Mum was obviously playing for time.

"Just someone," I said vaguely. I didn't want to mention Oscar's name, because if I did, I'd be duty bound to tell my mum that he was dead, and worse still, that he'd died violently.

"Frankly, Kylie," said Mum in a confidential tone, "the program was rather an embarrassment, so I didn't mention it."

I recalled that Oscar had thought it was called "Aussie Chicks Make Good." I asked Mum if that was the title.

"Something along those lines," she said. " 'Aussies O.S. Make Good,' I think it was, but it was a trashy show, not worthy of you, darl."

"How did they know about me in the first place?"

"Nephew Brucie," said Mum, obviously disgusted. "He took it upon himself to call the network when they ran an ad asking for stories of ordinary Aussies being successful overseas. And he supplied photos of you too. If I'd have known, I would've stopped him quick smart, but needless to say, Brucie wouldn't dream of checking with me."

Depressed though I was, a spark of interest made me ask, "Did you record the show?"

Silence. Then, "I might have."

"Will you send it to me, please?"

My mother reluctantly agreed. Now I was definitely interested in what the program contained. "What did it say about me, Mum?"

"Oh, I don't know…something about you going to L.A. to run a private investigation company," she said vaguely.

"Was it complimentary?"

She dodged that question by saying, "It wasn't accurate. For one thing, it said you were taking steps to become a private eye yourself."

"I am."

Silence. If it was something Mum really didn't want to hear, she ignored it. At last she said, "I have to admit the item about you was very short, like all the others, but it was rather flattering. You know how those TV types like to put a gloss on things."

Now I had an inkling of the devious motive that had kept my mum quiet about the program. "You didn't mention me being on TV because you thought it might influence me to stay in America. Is that right?"

"It may have crossed my mind."

"Crikey, Mum, you must think I'm shallow."

"Not shallow, Kylie darling, but anyone's head can be turned."

Any other time I would have had a bit of a barney with her over this, but last night I'd felt too down in the dumps to bother. We'd chatted for a few minutes longer about what was going on at the pub, then I'd made the excuse I was tired, and we'd rung off.

In the morning I didn't feel much better. I couldn't stomach breakfast, so I skipped my usual kitchen routine. Besides, I couldn't face talking to anyone yet, especially Melodie or Fran, who were no doubt still warring over Quip's play. Showered and dressed, I vowed to myself that today I'd make progress on the case. Ariana might not desire me as a lover, but she was going to admire me as a business partner, or I'd die in the attempt.

Before I left I went to my office to check my e-mail, in the hope that Diana Niptucker had replied to my message, but there was nothing from her. My cell phone rang just as I picked up my things to go out to the car.

"Kylie, it's Quip. I'm outside in the backyard. I need to see you desperately. And for God's sake, don't let Fran know I'm here."

When I pushed open the back door, a perfect morning greeted me, warm but not hot, full of sunshine and joyous nature...and an agitated Quip. "What's up?" I said.

"You know what's up!" He clutched my shoulder. "You've got to help me out, Kylie. Fran and Melodie are at daggers drawn—and I'm in the middle." His handsome face was contorted with anguish. "How could I have been so stupid?"

"Casting Fran was a bad idea?"

"Omigod, like, total disaster. What was I thinking!"

"They're both mad as cut snakes," I said, "but it'll blow over."

Quip's wide shoulders drooped—he had a crash-hot body from

going to the gym every day. "Fran's upset. Melodie's upset. Casting *Laughter Under Luna* is at a standstill…" He shook his head. "Being a playwright shouldn't be this much of a hassle. And I thought screenwriting was hard. Hello?"

I was sympathetic but had to get to work. Businesslike, I inquired, "Is there a part for Melodie?"

"Only Ethel/Ethelbert, and Melodie says that's a supporting role, not worthy of her talents."

"And you don't want to move Fran from Lucy/Lucas?"

Quip tossed off a mirthless laugh. "Move Fran? Not if I want to continue living." He gave me an earnest you-can-solve-it look. "I don't mind telling you, I'm tearing my hair out here. Help me, Kylie."

In my head I heard the Beach Boys singing, *Help, help, help me, Kylie.* I had to admit Rhonda sounded better. "Would you be willing to lie?" I asked Quip.

"Lie? I'd sell my firstborn, if I had one."

Melodie believes she's a bit psychic," I observed.

"Well, wow! That's a tremendous help," Quip said with a sardonic smile and a flip of his wrist. "I can't thank you enough."

Quip really was delightfully gay, but he and Fran seemed to have a happy marriage-if happy was ever a word one could associate with Fran.

I gave a quick glance at my watch. I couldn't be late two days in a row. "I really should go."

"Then leave!" he said, superdramatic, the back of his hand held to his brow. "But remember, my blood will be on your head!"

"Crikey, I couldn't cope with the guilt."

"So what's the plan?"

"You take Melodie aside and tell her you're speaking in the strictest confidence—and that Fran must never know what you are about to reveal."

"What am I about to reveal?" Quip asked.

"That you've never admitted it before, even to yourself, but there's a hidden, supernatural side to your creativity. When the inspiration of the play came to you, you had a dinkum psychic flash about the dynamics between the characters." I stopped to consider possibilities. "I reckon you could have been channeling the person who played Ethel in *I Love Lucy.*"

"Vivian Vance. She's dead."

"So you had this psychic link with Vivian Vance in the afterlife, and she set you straight." I repressed a smile. There was nothing straight about Quip. "All the time Lucy/Lucas thinks she/he is the main character, it's really Ethel/Ethelbert who's totally pivotal to the deep underlying themes." I paused briefly to do a quick edit. "Deep universal themes would be better."

Quip gave me a half-hopeful, half-doubtful look. "Go on."

"You haven't wanted to admit your psychic side to anyone, knowing you'd be mocked, but secretly you've been hoping Melodie would be willing to play Ethel/Ethelbert. That's why you cast Fran as Lucy/Lucas. You wanted to save the truly important role for Melodie."

Skeptical, Quip said, "And you think Melodie will swallow this?"

"Bonzer chance she will, as long as you remember to mention how talented she is." I didn't feel like a hypocrite saying this, because I'd seen Melodie use her acting abilities on several occasions-none of them onstage or on-camera—and she was talented.

"I can do that," declared Quip, enthused. "I'll make Melodie believe me." He gave me a big smile, showing the thousands of dollars for his tooth veneers had been well spent. "Hitchcock was right, you know. Actors are like children."

"Who are like children?" It was Fran, glowering from the back door. She switched her glare to me. "What are you doing out here with Quip?"

"He'll explain," I said, squeezing past her. "I really must go."

⊃

I'd just parked my car at UCLA and was on my way to the biology department, when my cell phone rang. It was Melodie. "Ariana asked me to tell you Dr. Penny's coming into the office at five-thirty today for a progress report. Ariana says if you can make it too, it'd be good."

I thanked Melodie and clicked off, mega-mopey. Ariana could have called me herself, but she clearly didn't want to speak with me. How depressing was that?

I drooped along for a bit, then straightened my shoulders. Bloody hell! I was going to show Ariana how I could solve a case single-handedly.

I was striding along when I heard, "Judy!" It was Clifford Van Horden III heading in my direction. "I've been looking for you everywhere," he said, his smoothly handsome face creased with chagrin that I'd been able to evade him.

"Been hiding from you," I said, quite truthfully. Frankly, I couldn't see what there was about me that was attracting this bloke. I certainly hadn't encouraged him in any way—quite the contrary.

Maybe that was it: Rejection was a turn-on for Clifford Van Horden III.

"Why have you been looking for me?" I inquired.

He treated me to a charming, luminescent smile. "Why does a man go looking for that one particular woman?" he asked roguishly.

"High hopes of mind-blowing sex?"

He blinked, simultaneously turning off his smile. Then he fired it up again. "I love it! You Aussies are so direct. It's refreshing. Different."

He went to put his arm around my waist, but I stepped nimbly out of reach. "I have an appointment," I said. "Urgent, vital, pressing. Must run."

"I'll walk you there."

"No need," I said, breaking into a trot. Van Horden III kept up quite easily.

"When will I see you again, Judy?" he asked. "Are you free this evening?"

"Sorry, no. Packed social schedule."

Too late I realized this was probably the wrong thing to say. His sort would want me all the more if he thought I was in demand.

"I don't give up easily," he said.

"I can see that."

If I'd had the time, I would have headed to some decoy building just so he wouldn't know where I was located on campus, but if I did that, I'd be late.

I skidded to a stop outside my destination, put out my hand and shook his. "Bonzer to see you again, Clifford Van Horden III."

"But—"

"I'll keep an eye out for you." And I would so I could avoid him.

When I reached Georgia Tapp's office, there was a long line of people waiting for assignments, chatting cheerfully to each other. The exception was Zoran Pestle, who was pacing up and down, his face dark.

Spying me, he came over to snarl, "The Tapp woman's too busy to deal with the likes of us. Typical! She's in with Yarrow. 'Urgent matters,' she said. It doesn't seem to occur to her that our time's valuable." He cast a searing look at the other members of staff, who, oblivious of his disapproval, were trading indecent jokes. "At least my time is."

Georgia herself appeared at Yarrow's door, her plump hands fluttering in agitation. She looked the perfect lady in her floral dress, sensible heels, and discreet jewelry. "So sorry, so sorry," she cried. "A most urgent procedural matter, most urgent."

She hurried into her office, reemerging a moment later with a sheaf of papers in her hand. "Today's schedule," she announced, distributing pages with alacrity. People began to wander off. "Speed is of the essence," she called after them. "So much remains to be done."

When she came to me, Georgia paused. "Ah, Kylie. Professor Yarrow wants to see you immediately."

"Right-oh."

Yarrow was sitting bolt upright behind his desk, his thin lips set in a tight line. He was not alone. Winona Worsack, medievally garbed, sat primly in a chair; Wally Easton's considerable bulk lounged against the windowsill.

Yarrow managed an excuse of a smile. "Kylie, sit down."

I nodded to the other two—both ignored me—and plunked myself in the chair he indicated. "What can I do for you, Prof?" I asked with a sunny smile.

No one returned it. Easton swiveled his shaved head to look out the window. Winona stared at me as though I were an insect on a slide. I checked out her wheels and was quite disappointed to find she actually had long, slender feet. Maybe there were tiny wheels attached to the soles of her shoes.

Yarrow seemed pained at my contraction of his title, but deciding to ignore it, he said, "You're on friendly terms with Erin Fogarty, and that's what she desperately needs at the moment, a friend. I'm hoping you'll help us keep an eye on her."

"I'm not sure what you mean."

Yarrow sighed. "Frankly, I'm very concerned about Erin. She called me last night at home, quite hysterical, saying the police believe she was the one who pushed Dr. Braithwaite off the roof."

"Crikey," I said. "Do you think she did?"

Winona Worsack broke in with a terse "It was an accident."

"Yes," said Yarrow, "a dreadful accident. But contrary to what Erin says, I'm afraid that she may well have been there when it happened. Apparently, she sent a text message to Braithwaite's phone, setting up the time and place."

"Doesn't sound good for her," I said.

Yarrow did a rueful head shake. "I'm afraid it doesn't, and I'm worried she's so stressed by the situation that she might do something stupid."

"Like what?" I asked, wide-eyed.

Yarrow looked very grave. "Hurt herself in some way."

"Commit suicide?"

My blunt words elicited a grimace from Yarrow and a sharp look from Winona, who said, "The girl's clearly emotionally unbalanced, but hardly suicidal. If we believed she was at risk, steps would be taken to admit her immediately to a hospital."

A monstrous idea was forming in my mind. Could it be that Yarrow intended to plant the idea that Erin might be suicidal, so that later she could be killed? And if her body was found with a note accepting responsibility for Oscar's death, so much the better.

"Maybe Erin does need to see a doctor," I said. "I'd be glad to go with her."

Over at the window, Easton turned his head to look at me. He had a flat, reptilian stare that prickled my skin.

"That won't be necessary," said Yarrow emphatically. "This morning I had a long, intimate chat with Erin, and she's calmed down considerably, knowing I'm taking a fatherly interest in her welfare."

I glanced at Winona, expecting she'd be browned off to have her husband burbling on about an intimate conversation with a female student, but Winona was impassive.

"Erin needs peer support," said Winona, who surely didn't give a brass razoo whether Erin had support or not. "We're asking you to be her friend. Let her talk things through. Find out what's she thinking. Help us to understand her problems."

"I reckon her main problem is she might be charged with murder."

Shaking his head, Yarrow got to his feet. "A tragic situation for everyone. We can only hope the authorities decide it was misadventure and nothing more." He made an attempt at a grateful smile. "Thank you so much, Kylie. I do appreciate your help with Erin. If you wouldn't mind, I'd appreciate it if at the end of each day you report how Erin is faring to my assistant, Ms Tapp."

"Right-oh."

He took my arm to lead me to the door. "And please, at any time I'm available if you have particular worries about Erin's welfare."

I glanced back to see Winona glowering at her husband. She clearly didn't trust him as far as she could throw him, and from the way he was massaging my arm with his fingers, she was right.

TWENTY-ONE

Georgia had put me back to work collating stuff for the symposium attendees, and when I got to the room, Erin was already there, wandering from desk to desk, listlessly collecting a page from each neat pile. Apart from us, the room was empty.

"G'day," I said.

"Oh, hi, Carol."

"Kylie."

"Sorry. Kylie."

For a change, she wasn't crying, but sniffs punctuated the silence every few moments. After a particularly loud sniff, Erin said to me, "Have the cops interviewed you yet?"

"About Dr. Braithwaite? Why would they want to? I don't know anything."

Erin's eyes immediately filled with tears. "You're lucky," she wailed. "I've been interviewed twice, and they don't believe me when I'm telling God's honest truth."

"That's rough," I said.

Erin grabbed my arm—she was turning into a bit of a clutcher. "You said I was being set up," she said, "and you were right. I told the detectives that Georgia Tapp was lying when she said she'd never spoken to me about Dr. Braithwaite, but they just said it was my word against hers."

"I'm sure they'll find out the truth in the end," I said soothingly.

"That's what Jack said this morning." Erin had given up any pretense of calling him Professor Yarrow. She released my arm to blow her nose on a tattered Kleenex. "Jack said he'd have a word with

Georgia, and find out what was going on."

"So he believes you. That's good."

Whoops! She'd re-clutched my arm, and her eyes were brimming with tears again. "He wants to," she cried, "he really does, but the scientist in him forces him to say he doesn't know what to believe."

"Let's go over it again," I said, "right from the very beginning, when you were working with Oscar Braithwaite in Australia…"

⊃

As instructed, before I left UCLA in the afternoon, I reported to Georgia. She was tapping away on her keyboard, and looked up with a rosy face when I knocked.

"Kylie! Come in." Obviously Yarrow had told her to be friendly and welcoming, because she bestowed a bright smile on me. "Professor Yarrow told me to expect you. You're here to report on Erin?"

I gave her back my warmest smile. "Crikey, you work hard," I said admiringly. "All that work organizing people for the Global Marsupial Symposium as well as keeping up with your own job—I don't know how you do it."

Georgia looked gratified. "Working for an eminent professor is demanding," she agreed. "But it's so rewarding." She gestured toward the papers beside her computer. "Truly, I feel I'm part of scientific history, setting down the words of the extraordinary keynote address Professor Yarrow will deliver to the symposium on Friday."

"The one on quokkas that Dr. Braithwaite was going to do?"

A shadow crossed her well-fed face. "Tragic death, of course, but almost like fate had stepped in to save Professor Yarrow from an unwarranted attack upon his reputation." She lay a hand flat on the pile of papers. "These contain the professor's groundbreaking and entirely original research. He's calling it 'The Quokka Question.'"

My eyes were riveted on the pages under her hand. This had to be the only existing version of Oscar's work, stolen by Yarrow. No doubt he'd rewritten some of it, but the basic elements would be the same. If I could only get my hands on those pages…but then I had nothing to compare them with. Erin had told me she'd destroyed all copies Oscar had before she'd left for the States.

"And how is little Erin Fogarty?" Georgia inquired. "Professor Yarrow is so worried about her emotional state."

"Bearing up surprisingly well under the circumstances." I'd decided no matter what state Erin was in, I'd give a positive report. I was working on the principle that Yarrow would not be inclined to fake a suicide, if that was his intention, while Erin appeared to be coping with the situation.

"Indeed?" said Georgia, rather surprised. "I gathered she was, as the saying goes, falling to pieces."

"She's rallied," I said. "I think Professor Yarrow taking an interest in her welfare has made her feel much better."

"It's so typical of the man," said Georgia, starry-eyed. I watched her stacking the pages I coveted and placing them in a folder. She closed the file on the computer, and turned it off. "Academic meeting," she said. "The professor likes me by his side, taking notes on important points."

She put the quokka folder in the bottom drawer of her desk, then locked with a key she took from the top drawer of her desk. This wasn't, I was pleased to observe, my idea of security.

Georgia picked up her notebook, pen, and purse; she ushered me out of her office and locked the door with a key she returned to her purse. Obviously, if I wanted a look at Yarrow's keynote address, it would have to be when the office door was open, perhaps sometime tomorrow.

⊃

I'd left plenty of time to get back to Kendall & Creeling for Pen's meeting with Ariana. For once, the traffic was flowing well, so I had twenty minutes to spare when I pulled into our parking area.

Fran was just about to clamber into her SUV. Naturally, it was one of those bulky, looming vehicles—would Fran have anything else?— so it was a struggle for someone as short as she was to make the driver's seat.

"Want a leg up?" I said.

Fran was preoccupied and didn't hear me. "Something's wrong with Melodie," she said.

"What sort of wrong?"

Fran gave me a puzzled scowl. "She's being nice to me."

"'Strewth, that is a worry."

"She actually said she was glad I was to play Lucy/Lucas. Can you believe it?"

I shook my head. "Amazing."

"Of course I asked Melodie why she'd had a change of heart. She said she'd had a psychic flash about the casting." Fran made a derisive sound. "Like, I believe that."

I shook my head again. "Strange things happen."

With an effort, Fran got herself into the SUV's driver's seat. She put down the window and leaned out to say, "Speaking of strange things, Quip told me what you two were talking about this morning."

"Oh?" I said, wondering what story he'd come up with.

She tossed off a scornful laugh. "Kylie, as if you could play Ethel/Ethelbert!"

"Quip told you I was aiming to audition for the part?"

"I had to drag it out of him, but yes."

"Hell's bells," I said, "you've got to aim high in life, you know, Fran. Fortunately, Quip let me down gently, pointing out this was way too high. He's a bonzer bloke."

Fran turned the ignition, and her behemoth roared to life. "Quip's all mine," she yelled above the noise. "Don't you ever forget it."

My smile faded as I ambled across the courtyard to the front door. In a few minutes I'd face Ariana, and I wasn't sure how I'd cope. She'd be chilly toward me; that was certain. I'd forced her to tell me something so deeply personal that each word must have hurt. Then I berated myself. Why right did I have to whinge? Ariana was the one with tragedy in her life, not me. Perhaps she feared there'd be pity in my eyes. I was sure she would hate that as much as I would.

I opened the front door with unaccustomed reluctance, not knowing how I should behave when I went to Ariana's office. Perhaps I should wait until Pen arrived for the meeting. It would be much easier with someone else there, and we could all concentrate on the case.

Melodie, in place at the reception desk, leaped up when she saw me. Rushing over, she exclaimed, "Kylie, you'll never guess what's happened!" She looked around with elaborate care. "It's confidential. Are we alone?"

"Unless someone's crouched behind your desk, I reckon we are."

"Fran must never know," she whispered.

"Better not to tell me then. Fran's the sort who could get blood out of a stone, so extracting a secret from this little Aussie would be child's play for her."

Clearly disappointed, Melodie said, "But it's about *LUL*."

"OK, then, I'm all ears. Fran's already got the main part, so she won't care about anything else."

"But that's it!" said Melodie, flashing wide green eyes at me. "She only thinks she's got the main part."

"How come?"

"Quip's real psychic, the same as me." Melodie looked mysterious. "I can't reveal the details, but like, Quip's had a vision from a crossover."

"A pedestrian walkway?"

Melodie frowned at my less-than-serious attitude. "Very funny, Kylie. A crossover is someone who's crossed over."

"Seems logical."

"Have you got it yet?" She was growing impatient. "Dead and gone. Speaking from the other side."

"I reckon I've got it. Pushing up daisies. Kicked the bucket. Carked it. Done a perish."

Melodie sighed. "Sometimes you're just so hard to get through to, Kylie."

"Sorry. Must come from being an Aussie."

"That must be it," she agreed. "Anyhow, as I was saying, Quip had this mystic moment, when he realized the major, pivotal character in *LUL* is Ethel/Ethelbert—the one who expresses the essence of the deep universal themes that permeate the play."

"Fair dinkum?"

"Of course it's true," she snapped. "Why would I be telling you otherwise?"

"So who'll be playing Ethel/Ethelbert? Ashlee, maybe?"

"Ashlee? No way." Melodie tapped herself on the chest. "Me."

"Blimey, I can see why you don't want Fran to know. She's convinced she's snaffled the main part."

Melodie treated me to a view of her perfect dental equipment. "Good, isn't it?" she said.

ↄ

I chickened out and went to my own office. I told myself it was to check my e-mail, but I knew it was to avoid seeing Ariana by myself. E-mail checked and still no message back from Diana Niptucker, I was steeling myself to face Ariana when I heard the booming voice of Pen Braithwaite echoing down the hall. *Saved by the bell.*

I met her outside Ariana's black, brass-studded door. Impulsively, I gave Pen a hug, standing on tiptoes to achieve it. "Pen, how are you?"

"Coping, Kylie, coping." She seemed to have regained some of her former vitality, but her face was pale and her expression drawn. "I'll feel better when the bastard who killed Oscar is behind bars. I'm hoping you're making progress."

"Working at it. Do you know a Diana Niptucker? There was a something about her in Oscar's envelope."

"Di? I've known her for years. Small, dumpy woman, with a mind sharp as a razor. Oscar admired her iconoclastic take on things." Pen added approvingly, "She stirs up controversy wherever she goes. The Aussie megafauna mafia hate Di with a passion."

"I've e-mailed her, but she hasn't got back to me."

"Out in the field, probably. Di gets obsessed, and doesn't bother much with eating, sleeping, and the like. She spends most of her life scrabbling round in rocks looking for fossils." Pen snorted with a shadow of her usual flamboyance. "Nitpicking stuff. I'd never do it. Give me warm bodies and hot sex any day."

Lonnie, folder under one arm, had appeared while she was speak-

165

ing. "My philosophy exactly," he said with lascivious grin, "warm bodies and hot sex." His smile faded as he looked up into Pen's face. Giving her hand an awkward pat, he mumbled, "Sorry. Things are tough, I know."

She nodded mutely. Lonnie shuffled his feet. To break the uncomfortable silence, I said, "You're joining our meeting, Lonnie?"

"Yeah, I've got a few things to report on Pen's stalker."

We crowded into Ariana's office. I was careful not to meet Ariana's eyes, having the conviction if she looked into mine, she'd see the utter misery there.

Once we were all settled—Ariana behind her desk, Pen and I seated on the other side, Lonnie perched on the edge of his chair between us—Ariana gave a summary of the police investigation so far.

"I talked to Ted Lark this afternoon. As we were LAPD colleagues in the past, he was willing to discuss the case with me."

Pen didn't seem impressed. "Detective Lark and his offsider have interviewed me twice. Don't have a lot of time for Lark. Right away, I made it plain who was responsible for Oscar's murder, but he wouldn't even admit it was a homicide. I set him straight on the plagiarism, I pointed out how much Jack Yarrow had to lose. I practically did his bloody job for him, but all your precious detective friend would say was that he was investigating every aspect of the case."

"That's all he can say at this point," said Ariana mildly.

"And I asked Lark a heap of questions," said Pen in a tone of extreme exasperation, "but did he answer them? No! He wouldn't even give me the time of Oscar's death."

"It was between seven and ten on Saturday night," said Ariana. "A canvass of staff and students hasn't turned up anyone who saw Oscar near the building at or near that time frame, and there were no witnesses to the fall."

"On Saturday evening, that part of the campus is like a graveyard," said Pen. She grimaced, realizing what she'd said.

"It's preliminary only," said Ariana, "but the coroner's office confirms Oscar died of blunt-force trauma, sustained when he hit the ground. There was evidence, however, of a blow to the back of his skull that probably occurred just a few minutes before death."

"So he could've been unconscious when he fell?" Pen looked almost relieved. "I've been visualizing what must have gone through Oscar's mind in those last seconds. It's a slight comfort to think he didn't know he was about to die."

Ariana continued, reviewing the crime scene investigation, saying there'd been nothing of note on the roof of the building, nor in the area where Oscar's body had landed. As for Oscar himself, there was no evidence he'd defended himself against an attacker. Nor were their any unusual fibers or other materials on his clothes or body.

"The perfect crime," said Pen bitterly.

"That's unlikely," said Ariana. "If it were perfect, there'd be no questions asked at all. As it is, Erin Fogarty raises quite a few."

I spoke for the first time since entering the room. "I spent a lot of time with Erin today, and I've got some new information."

"Can I get my stalker stuff done first?" said Lonnie. "I've got to get back to set up a surveillance for Bob."

He flipped open the folder he'd been holding. "It's all here, but I can give it to you in a couple of sentences."

"Since the call to my show on Saturday, I've haven't had a thing from the guy," said Pen.

"If he goes to ground, that'll make him close to impossible to find," said Lonnie. "What we've got now is zero, since Pen destroyed his written notes, and he hasn't been obliging enough to turn up on the surveillance camera I set up at the apartment. I sent Harriet to quiz any florists Pen recalled, but no one had any reason to remember who arranged for the flowers to be delivered, and cash transactions leave no paper trail."

"What about the calls to my program?" said Pen. "Aren't there voiceprints, or something like that?" She glared at Ariana, as though it were Ariana's fault. "Blasted Lark wasn't the slightest interested in my stalker. I even gave him Wally Easton's name. Lark said he'd investigate, but I doubt he'll bother. He told me it didn't appear to him to have anything to do with Oscar's death."

"I've listened to the calls," said Lonnie. "Voiceprints would probably implicate Easton, if it's his voice, but what does it prove? Only that he made unpleasant telephone calls to you, and your program provokes that type of response from some people. He never mentions your brother. There's no evidence to link him to any crime."

As Pen subsided, muttering something about police corruption, Lonnie got up. He patted Pen's shoulder, muttered, "See you later," and left the room.

After the door had closed behind him, Ariana said firmly, "There's no corruption, Pen. I've known Ted Lark for years. He's a thorough, reliable investigator. I would trust him to follow the evidence wherever it leads him. But that's the point. Is there evidence pointing to a suspect? All the suspicion in the world means nothing without hard facts."

"What about Erin Fogarty?" Pen demanded. "Isn't there evidence to implicate her in luring Oscar to his death?"

"Her cell phone certainly was used to send the text message to Oscar's phone, setting up the rendezvous at the building site."

"Yarrow told her to do it," snarled Pen. "The bastard. Once it was set up, Yarrow kept the appointment with Oscar—and murdered him."

"When Erin Fogarty was interviewed," said Ariana, "she repeated everything she'd already told Kylie. She laid all the blame on Georgia Tapp, and defended Jack Yarrow, saying she was sure he knew nothing about the scheme. Erin became hysterical when Lark confronted her with the text message sent from her cell phone to Oscar's. She swore the only thing she did was to tell Oscar on Friday afternoon to watch out for a message she'd send about meeting him the next day. That's all. According to Erin, it must have been Georgia Tapp who messaged Oscar."

Her skepticism obvious, Pen said, "So how does Erin account for her phone being used to send it?"

"She maintains Georgia Tapp must have borrowed her phone without telling her. She says she couldn't find her cell on Friday, and thought she'd mislaid it somewhere, but then discovered the phone sitting on her desk in the biology department when she came in Monday morning."

"And Lark believes this preposterous story?"

"He's reserving judgment. Not surprisingly, when Georgia Tapp was interviewed, she announced the phone story was a total fantasy, the product of a sick mind, as was the whole fanciful account of how Erin had been co-opted to set Oscar up."

"And Yarrow? He's the milk-white innocent too?" Pen said.

Ariana's smile was sardonic. "Yarrow says he knows nothing about the whole sorry affair, but he's shocked that Erin should accuse his assistant, Georgia, who's taken a motherly interest in the young woman's welfare. Yarrow also volunteered how in recent weeks he's become extremely concerned about Erin's mental stability. He'd mentioned to his wife how Erin had formed an unhealthy attachment to him, even persuading herself that there was a sexual relationship between them. This, Yarrow assured Ted Lark, did not exist, but was entirely a product of a deranged mind."

I said, "I think that at every opportunity Yarrow is planting the idea that Erin is unbalanced so that when she apparently kills herself, no one will be all that surprised."

"So Erin Fogarty's the sacrificial lamb?" said Ariana.

"I reckon so." I recounted this morning's conversation with Jack Yarrow and Winona, and how Wally Easton had silently observed.

Pen was thoughtful. "Oscar was always on about Jack Yarrow, but I believe the really poisonous one is Winona Worsack. One look at her career and you'll realize she's a ruthless, cold bitch. Nothing and no one gets in her way. She'd definitely take any threat to Yarrow's academic standing as a personal affront."

"The Lady Macbeth type?" I said.

"Exactly."

"Erin thinks Yarrow's wife hates her because Yarrow and Erin are in love," I said.

This got a contemptuous snort from Pen. "Everyone in the faculty knows Yarrow goes through female graduates like a hot knife through butter. Erin Fogarty's just another besotted idiot. Winona wouldn't bother hating her."

"She's been very useful to the Yarrows," I said. "I encouraged Erin to tell me every little detail, starting from when she was out in the field studying quokkas with Oscar in Western Australia. She not only stole every copy of Oscar's research notes for Yarrow, before she left for the States, she destroyed the hard drive on Oscar's computer so there was no electronic version either."

Pen looked morose. "Oscar wouldn't hear anything against Erin Fogarty. He continued to have feelings for her, even though she betrayed him in the worst possible way."

"She did it for love," I said. "Jack Yarrow actually flew to Australia and met up with her in person. He persuaded Erin that Oscar was the one who had stolen his research."

"She's a credulous fool."

I had to agree with Pen. "She didn't even question the extra incentive Georgia Tapp gave her to use on Oscar if he balked at the idea of a secret meeting."

"Which was?" said Ariana.

"Erin was to say she'd overheard something about Dr. Penny and a stalker and that she thought she could find out more before tomorrow night. From what she says, Oscar would have met her anyway, but that was the final clincher."

"Jesus!" said Pen, dabbing at her eyes, "That was what Oscar meant when he told me he had a lead on my stalker. And I laughed at him..."

To switch to another subject before she broke down, I said, "My theory is that the meeting between Erin and Oscar on Friday in the parking structure was deliberately set up at that location so there was an excellent chance she'd be seen with him."

It worked: rage flooded Pen's face. "Jack Yarrow believes he's thought of everything, that it's working out just the way he planned." She leaned over, seized my shoulder and actually shook me. "Kylie, the ball's in your court. Bring the bastard down!"

⊃

After I'd seen Pen off, I came back inside full of purpose. I'd go to Ariana and say something about last night. I wasn't sure what it would be, but I'd play it by ear and hope for the best.

I had a moment's amusement at these two clichés, beloved by my mum, but then I squared my shoulders and walked quickly to Ariana's door before I could change my mind.

She opened it as I put my hand on the latch. "Kylie, I was just coming to see you."

"Your office or mine?"

She smiled faintly. "Yours, I think."

We walked in silence down the hall. Once there, I didn't take shelter behind my desk, but sat down opposite her at the low coffee table.

"Ariana, about last night—"

"I shouldn't have been so hard on you, Kylie, at the end."

She was calm and contained as always, but the stress showed in her voice. I gazed at her face, her dear face, and said, "Please forgive me, Ariana. It was I who was hard on you. You knew I'd never give up until you told me."

"Will you give up now?"

"Give up what? My share of Kendall & Creeling? Or give up you? I haven't got you, Ariana, so there's nothing to give up."

She looked away from me. "If things could be different..."

A dreadful feeling of loss flooded through me. "But they're not. I understand that."

She brought her blue laser eyes back to me. "So where do we go from here?"

I fought to keep my voice steady. "As friends? Colleagues."

"Can you do that?"

"I can do that," I said.

TWENTY-TWO

At three-thirty in the morning, Diana Niptucker called. The office number, as usual, was switched through to the phone on my bedside table. I was startled awake by the noise of its ring, which sounded so much louder in the darkness. Groping around, I found the handset and mumbled a hello.

"Kylie? Kylie Kendall? This is Di Niptucker, calling from Australia." Her voice was brisk.

I sat up, disturbing Julia Roberts, who'd been dozing by my side. "Dr. Niptucker! Thank you for getting in touch with me."

"What time is it there in the States?"

I squinted at the illuminated dial of my bedside clock. "Around three-thirty in the morning."

"Oh, then I woke you. Sorry, but I just picked up my e-mails, and saw your message. Been incommunicado at a dig in the middle of nowhere for weeks, and have just got back to civilization. Had no idea what was going on in the world. Oscar's gone, is he? Dead?"

"Yes, I'm afraid so."

"Shame. Talented man. We were intending to publish a joint paper on the quokka megafauna link."

"Titled 'The Quokka Question'?"

Di Niptucker gave a snort of laughter. "Good grief, no. That was Oscar's name for it, but I, of course, would have insisted on the correct scientific language, both in the title and in the body of the paper. No point in dumbing down things, that's what I say. I believe 'The Quokka Question' was what he was calling his keynote address to the GMS, however."

172

A hope sprang to life. "Dr. Niptucker, if you were writing a joint paper with Oscar Braithwaite, perhaps you had some of his latest quokka research notes."

"All of them," said Di Niptucker. "I insisted on it. Oscar had a fine mind, but he was scatterbrained with it. No telling if he'd include everything relevant, so I asked for a copy of all his recent research."

"I think I'd better tell you what's been happening here," I said. I gave her a brief outline of the situation, and she listened without a single interruption, until I mentioned my suspicions about Jack Yarrow and Oscar's death.

"Revolting man," she snapped. "I know him. Academic fraud. Capable of anything."

"If we had a copy of Oscar's research notes, they could be compared to the material Professor Yarrow is using for his keynote address this Friday."

"Say no more," she said. "What's your fax number?"

After I'd given it to her, Di Niptucker said, "I'll send them straight away. And keep me posted. I'd love to see Yarrow cut off at the knees."

After I'd thanked her and she'd hung up, I bolted out of bed and went to check that the fax machine had plenty of paper. Jules took this as an indication it was time for breakfast, so I indulged her with six prawn pieces and made a cup of tea for myself while I waited for the pages to come through.

I took my mug with me and watched greedily as the fax machine spat out each page of Oscar's research notes. They were indubitably genuine, as Di Niptucker had scrawled across the top of the facing page: "Comments in spidery handwriting mine. Illegible writing, Oscar's."

When the last page had been faxed, I gathered them up and took the bundle back to the kitchen. Reading through it I found much was double Dutch to me, but the structure and headings were enough to provide a template against which I could compare Yarrow's material for his address.

I couldn't even think of going back to bed. I photocopied every page twice, put one set in the office safe and the other on Ariana's desk. The faxed pages I put in a large envelope to take to UCLA with me.

Ariana wouldn't be in until mid morning, as she was seeing a prospective client. Perhaps I should call her and tell her what Dr. Niptucker had supplied: the evidence giving Yarrow an excellent motive for murder. But Ariana was likely to tell me to hold off until she saw the pages herself, and time was of the essence. I knew where Yarrow's notes were, and if Georgia's office was unlocked, I could get to them easily.

As my mother would say, strike while the iron is hot.

⊃

The campus was barely waking up when I arrived. I'd left Ariana a note clipped to her copy of the faxed pages that outlined the situation and told her what I intended to do. This made me feel better. I might not have called her, but I did tell her what was going on.

It was so early I had to kill time drinking coffee in the student union, but at last the hands of my watch crawled around to a reasonable hour, and clutching my precious envelope, I set off on my quest.

The biology department was deserted, and the door to Georgia's office was closed, indicating she hadn't yet arrived. I tried the handle anyway and was surprised when the door opened. I hadn't thought of the cleaning staff. Perhaps they unlocked the doors every morning to empty the wastepaper baskets.

I slipped in, closing the door behind me. I checked, but there was no way to lock it from inside the room. It took only a moment to find the key to the bottom drawer of the desk and take out the pages Georgia had been working on yesterday.

I sat down in her chair and opened the envelope I'd brought with me. My plan was to do a quick comparison and, if the similarities looked convincing, to call the UCLA Campus Police and tell them I'd discovered stolen scientific papers in Georgia Tapp's office. The officers would certainly confiscate all the pages until the matter was investigated, which would effectively stop Jack Yarrow from disposing of damning evidence.

It was quite silent, the only sound the pages as I flicked through them, looking for correspondences. And they were there, over and over.

It seemed Yarrow had lifted Oscar's work word for word, convinced it was safe to do so, as he held the only copy of the research.

My heart lurched as the door to the office opened with a soft snickering sound. I expected to see Georgia, but it was Winona Worsack who stood there, a look of cold surprise on her face.

"I'm waiting for Georgia," I said, "and catching up on research for my paper with Dr. Wasinsky."

She nodded as if convinced and closed the door again. I frantically collected the faxed pages, cramming them into the envelope. I looked around for something to conceal Yarrow's notes in, and found a manila folder. Better to call the campus cops from Rube's office—I'd feel safer there.

I'd got to my feet, stuffing the material for Yarrow's address into the folder, when the door opened again, and Jack Yarrow stepped in. His high, domed forehead was beaded with sweat. "What are you doing here?"

"Waiting for Georgia."

He looked at the folder in my hand, at the half-open drawer of Georgia's desk, and his eyes widened. "Give me that!" he said, attempting to snatch the folder from me. Pages cascaded to the floor.

"Pick them up," he said, "and give them to me."

Playing for time, I bent down to retrieve the pages. As I did so, Yarrow picked up my envelope and ripped it open. He clearly recognized the contents immediately. "Christ! Where did you get this?"

I shrugged, all the while desperately trying to find a way out. *I could push past him and run.* But that would leave the evidence with him, so I should snatch up as many of the papers as possible, and then get out of there. *I could—*

I saw with total astonishment that Yarrow was now holding a gun. Small and silver, it seemed impossibly melodramatic. "You're going to shoot me?" I said, incredulously.

"Indeed I will, unless you do exactly what I say."

I couldn't believe he was serious. "I'm not keen," I said. "Let's call the whole thing off."

"Amusing," said Yarrow, stone-faced. "We're going to walk out of the building together and make our way to the nearest parking structure. Nothing will be out of the ordinary. It'll all be very smooth, very calm."

Behind him, the door opened yet again. This time it was Georgia Tapp. She bustled into the room, then stopped dead, her mouth open, when she saw the gun. "Professor Yarrow!"

"Everything's under control, Georgia."

She'd gone a pasty whitish-gray, probably the color I was too. "Professor Yarrow," she repeated, this time as a whisper.

Sweat was running down his face. He licked his lips. "Forget you saw this, Georgia. Kylie and I will be leaving in a moment, and you must carry on as though nothing has happened. Can I trust you do that?"

Georgia just stared at him.

"That's asking a bit much of an administrative assistant," I said.

"Shut up," he snapped at me. To Georgia he said, "Go into my office and wait there. I'll be back shortly and explain everything to you."

She ducked her head in a quick nod, then scuttled out of her office. He jerked his head at me. "Your turn. Start moving."

"And if I don't cooperate?"

"I'll kill you. It won't be convenient, but Georgia will back me up. She'll agree you burst into my office, frenzied, this gun in your hand. Incidentally, it cannot be traced to me. In fear of my life, I struggled with you for the weapon. It went off. Tragically, you died instantly."

I said, "Make a bit of a mess of your carpet."

He regarded the floor pensively. "True, but carpet can always be replaced." Suddenly peeved, he snapped, "Look, I didn't want to get involved in all this violence. It's been forced upon me. First Oscar Braithwaite with his wild accusations. Now you."

"Seems to me if I agree to do what you say, you'll take me somewhere more convenient, and then kill me."

Yarrow pasted a sincere expression on his face. "I assure you that's not my intention. I merely want you out of commission until the Global Marsupial Symposium concludes. Then it won't matter. No one will listen to the ravings of an unbalanced graduate student determined to get revenge when I spurned your advances."

"If that's the case, why spirit me away? According to you, no one will pay any attention to me anyway."

His smile was cold. "Sophistry will get you nowhere." He gestured with the gun. "Turn around."

"Crikey," I said, "you must think I came down in the last shower. I'm not going anywhere."

His face became a hard mask. "Listen, you bitch," he ground out, "you've got two choices. Walk out on your own two feet right now, or be dragged out, unconscious, in the middle of the night. The first gives you the opportunity to stay in one piece. The second means I'll have to beat you unconscious—an unappealing option—and stash you under my desk until I can arrange to have your body collected."

"Do you have duct tape handy to restrain me if I wake up?"

That got me a wintry smile. "Indeed I do."

"I'll take the walking option," I said. I didn't believe for a nanosecond that Yarrow had any intention of letting me live, but at least I'd have some slight chance of getting away from him if we were out in the open air.

My *Complete Handbook* noted that most people were dreadful shots, especially with handguns, and that it was preferable to run and take your chances, rather than allow yourself to be put into a vehicle.

I was prepared to do this, but as soon as we were out of Georgia's office, Yarrow locked one arm around my shoulders, and rammed the gun against my ribs with his other hand, his jacket coat hiding it from view. We strolled like lovers down the hall, clattered down the steps, and outside into the warm morning air. My heart was hammering and I felt light-headed. Perhaps I could pretend to faint? Perhaps he'd shoot me, if I did.

"Let me make this very clear," he said, once we were on the wide concrete walkway leading to the parking structure. "If you cooperate, nothing unpleasant will happen to you."

He emphasized this comment with a sharp jab of the barrel into my ribs. "Winona is waiting for us at the car. When I give the word, you will climb into the trunk. Winona will drive you to a friend's place. You'll be his guest until after the symposium. You'll be quite safe. Nothing will happen to you."

"This friend wouldn't be Wally Easton, would it?"

He was momentarily surprised, then smiled thinly at me. "How perspicacious of you, my dear. I'm sure you'll enjoy his particular brand of hospitality. I must warn you, however, not to rile Wally. He can be impulsive, I'm afraid."

The thought of being in Wally Easton's clutches was too horrible to contemplate. I looked around, frantic to find some way out before I lost any option to escape. There were a few students around but no one close to us.

"Don't do anything stupid," Yarrow hissed. He tightened his arm around my shoulder. "Try something and I'll pull the trigger. I won't hesitate."

We were getting dangerously close to the parking structure. I had to do something—now. I'd take my chances at being shot. Anything was better than the fate Yarrow intended for me.

"Judy! Hey, Judy! Over here!"

Twenty meters away stood Clifford Van Horden III, cast in the unlikely role of my knight in shining armor.

While Yarrow swiveled his head, obviously wondering where the hell this Judy was, I summoned up what I hoped was an alluring smile. "Cliff! Darling! I've been looking for you everywhere!"

The "darling!" did it. He came rocketing over. "Here I am, Judy, ready and willing."

"Meet Professor Jack Yarrow," I said politely. "He's intending to murder me."

Clifford Van Horden III blinked at this but still thrust out his hand. "Pleased to meet you, sir."

"He's got a gun," I yelled, breaking Yarrow's hold on me.

My would-be rescuer's eyes were wide. "A gun?" he said, shrinking back. Not hero material at all.

As though I rehearsed it every day, a move from my self-defense course at the Wollegudgerie Police Club came back to me. With every bit of strength I could muster, I whacked Yarrow across the bridge of his nose with the side of my hand, then jabbed him in both eyes with my extended fingers. Blood spurted from his nose; he fell to his knees, the silver gun spinning away from him.

I became aware that Clifford Van Horden III was gazing at me, openmouthed. "Judy," he said at last. "Judy!"

TWENTY-THREE

I'd broken a bone in my hand and had bruised ribs from being poked by the gun barrel, so I was in some pain, but it was nothing to the pain Jack Yarrow was feeling. Not only had I fractured his nose and given him two black eyes, but his faithful administrative assistant was singing, as Lonnie said, like a yellow canary. Yarrow had been arrested on suspicion of murder, and Winona and Easton were under intensive investigation with charges likely to follow.

Pen Braithwaite came close to snapping my bruised ribs with a huge hug; Di Niptucker sent congratulations from Australia; even my mother admitted I'd done a bonzer job. Everyone at Kendall & Creeling was pleased with me, except Ariana. Oh, she commended me for solving the case of the quokka question, but it was cool praise. A chilly curtain seemed to have come down between us.

Fran chose this point to stage a surprise disaster drill. Everyone was involved: Ariana, Bob, Melodie, Lonnie, Harriet, me, and, of course, Fran herself. The drill did not go well. Fran was seriously displeased with us, observing acidly that if this had been a genuine terrorist attack or natural catastrophe, we would all be stone-cold dead.

Her main ire was directed toward Lonnie, who had finally got his gas mask in place and was doing a jerky robot-walk while repeating "Take me to your leader" in a machine-voice monotone.

It really was funny, and we all laughed, except for Fran. She smacked Lonnie across the side of the head with a first aid kit, no doubt to jolt some sense into him, but it had the opposite effect. Lonnie did a theatrical swan dive and thrashed around on the floor, saying, "System crash! System crash!"

Even Ariana had tears in her eyes from laughter, and Bob, who when keenly amused, gave out the most disconcerting, braying cackle and came close to choking. Fran, her hands on her hips, surveyed us stone-faced until we had laughed ourselves out.

"Wonderful," she said. "Brilliant. I'm calling a repeat drill at five o'clock. Perhaps by then the importance of disaster preparedness will have sunk in."

"We can't," said Melodie, still giggling. "Tonight's the play reading. We've got main parts, Fran. We have to leave early."

That wiped the smiles off several faces. This evening there was to be a reading of Quip's *Laughter Under Luna* in front of an invited audience. Quip had called each one of us to make sure we would definitely be attending. Harriet had shamelessly played the pregnancy card, saying her need for regular bathroom stops would be too disruptive to an audience grappling with an intensely dark tragedy.

The rest of us had no escape, although I halfheartedly tried the fact I had a damaged hand as an excuse. It didn't work: Quip had begged, and I'd given in. Having been exposed to the lines Melodie and Fran had been learning, I had the gloomy conviction we were all in for a very long night.

As convictions go, this one turned out to be only partly accurate. We all dutifully arrived at the theater, which was small, shabby, and cramped, and joined the other members of the audience, none of whom seemed particularly enthusiastic. I did my level best to snaffle a seat next to Ariana but was foiled by Lonnie on one side and a total stranger on the other.

Settling in my singularly uncomfortable seat, I recalled that Harriet had said that Quip intended *LUL* to distill the angst of the early twenty-first century. She'd been laughing when she'd said it, and as the reading began, I saw why. Quip had unintentionally written a funny deep tragedy.

The muffled giggles started almost immediately. Full belly laughs took a little longer. On the stage, Fran, Melodie, and the rest of the cast, all arrayed on high stools with leather-bound copies of *LUL* in their hands, seemed more puzzled than upset.

Melodie, apparently believing the levity had been caused by some lack of depth in performance, upped her lines to such searing intensity that the audience howled. So it turned out to be a long evening, but definitely an entertaining one.

In the crush after the performance, I looked for Ariana, but she had slipped away and no doubt was on her way home. For one mad moment I thought of getting in my car and following her there. I had a fair idea why she was giving me the cold shoulder and needed to have it out with her.

Good sense prevailed, and I returned to Julia Roberts instead. I went to bed, brooding. My hand hurt, my ribs hurt, my heart hurt. Jules inconsiderately had a full-scale wash on the bed around three o'clock in the morning. All in all, it was a miserable night.

I got up early, went into Ariana's room, and left a note on her desk. I'd labored over the wording for ages, trying several versions out on Julia Roberts. With her help, I'd finally ended up with the simple, "We need to talk."

People arrived. The day began. About nine-thirty Ariana came into my office. Shutting the door behind her she said, "That was reckless of you. Irresponsible."

"Rash," I said. "Impulsive."

"Don't laugh at me, Kylie. I'm serious. The first rule you learn in law enforcement is backup. You went in alone."

"I had to."

"You didn't."

"OK," I said, getting up and coming over to her. "I wanted to impress you. Prove to you I could be a crash-hot P.I., a worthy partner in the business. Maybe I went a bit far—"

Ariana gave a rueful half laugh. "I'm not altogether sure I can take the stress of having you as a partner."

"Do you notice a flock of little pink pigs circling the room, their tiny wings flapping?"

"I don't believe so."

"Until you do, I'm not going anywhere."

"I see."

"And I'm not hanging around expecting you to ever fall for me in any big way." I couldn't resist adding, "A small way would do, if you could manage it."

"Kylie…"

"And if you're counting on me losing interest and giving up, you've got Buckley's."

Up went her eyebrow. "And Buckley's would be?"

"Buckley's chance, which is no chance at all. You're stuck with me, Ariana."

"I'll try to cope."

"And I won't stop loving you, no matter what."

Ariana looked at me for a long moment. "I wouldn't want you to," she said.

ABOUT CLAIRE MCNAB

Claire McNab is the author of the detective-inspector
Carol Ashton and the undercover agent Denise Cleever
series. Like the star of her new series, Kylie Kendall,
Claire left her native Australia to live in Los Angeles, a
city she still finds quite astonishing.